YOU CAN'T RUN FOREVER

Valerie Koski

TO SOW IS TO HARVEST

Scythe Publications, Inc.

A Division of Winston-Derek Publishers Group, Inc.

First printing

Scripture quotes include:

Revised Berkeley Version, copyright 1945, Gerrit Verkuhl. Assigned 1958 Zondervan Publishing House.

Revised Standard Version, copyright 1946, Zondervan Publishing House.

New International Version, copyright 1973, International Bible Society.

PUBLISHED BY SCYTHE PUBLICATIONS, INC.
Nashville, Tennessee 37205

Library of Congress Catalog Card No: 92-56937
ISBN: 1-55523-580-8

Printed in the United States of America

To Kimberly, Katelyn, Kenneth, Kyle,
and especially Bill—for all your hard work.

Acknowledgements

I would like to gratefully acknowledge the contributions of the following people: Julieanne Alzate, Julie Carlson, Barb Crozier, Karla Friend, Richard Haggstrom, Jean Koski, Matt Ludwig, Jodi Morris, Regina Mulder, Ann Pederson, Bill Schaefer, Fay Schaefer, Linda Van Der Werf.

PROLOGUE 1

THE SIGN FOR THE BOULEVARD DRUGSTORE SHONE AHEAD. Its pink light cast a rosy glow around the entrance as Simon Felder approached the door. He had passed by several similar stores and signs while walking along L.A.'s Wilshire Boulevard.

Simon glanced at his watch. *8:45. These new hours are convenient,* he thought as he pulled the door open and stepped inside, leaving the chill of the November evening air behind. The small pharmacy was empty except for Bob, a pharmacist who had worked there as long as Simon could remember, and a young clerk whom Simon did not recognize.

Daniel, his nine year-old, had come home from school complaining of an earache. No doubt Rose would be bringing Daniel to the doctor the next day, but in the meantime a new heating pad would help him to sleep more comfortably. Rose had located the existing heating pad, but found it to be crumpled to the point of being unusable. When confronted with the mangled pad, her youngest two sons rather fearfully admitted to towing each other about the house on it.

Simon worked long hours at his restaurant, and this evening was no exception. Even though tomorrow was a Saturday, he would be unable to accompany Rose and the boys to the synagogue. He tried to help out when he could, but Rose ended up with the bulk of the family and household responsibilities. After a late dinner, however, he offered to run the errand for her. Rose had wanted him to drive, but Simon put his hands on his stomach and said, "If I don't start getting some exercise, people are going to start asking you who your new husband is!"

Simon walked down the aisle looking for his intended purchase. The pharmacist was putting items away in preparation for closing and the clerk put her jacket on, having already closed down the front cash register.

"I'll see you Monday, Bob!" she called, walking toward the rear exit.

"Have a good trip to your mother's tomorrow, Julie," returned the pharmacist with a slight wave of his hand as the clerk walked out.

Having found the object of his search, Simon paused in front of the magazine rack. With a few minutes left before 9 p.m., he had just enough time to find some new reading material.

Simon glanced up as he heard someone enter the drugstore. A teenager looked around, then sauntered cockily down the main aisle. He was at that in-between age of being neither boy nor man.

Which one to choose? Simon asked himself as he studied the three magazines that looked most interesting. Although he wanted all three, Rose had reminded him before he left that their checkbook was running low. Trying to keep out of the pharmacist's way, he reached for a magazine of games and puzzles.

Simon was aware of the other customer walking slowly down the aisle, and then suddenly quickening his stride as if coming to a decision.

"Both of you—get in the back of the store! Right now!"

Simon looked up and saw the teen pointing a pistol at them. Fear shot through Simon's body as the magazines dropped from his fingers. The pharmacist spun around and took a step forward before noticing the gun.

"I want cash, everything you have. If you try anything—I'll shoot!"

The pharmacist turned pale and with shaking hands went to open the back cash register.

"Move it!" the teen said to Simon, motioning with his gun. He nervously stepped back as if unsure who to aim his gun at. Suddenly, his foot caught a display rack, and the youth fell to the floor, his pistol flying just out of his reach. Simon saw his chance, and without even thinking he lunged for the gun. The teen tried to push him away, but Simon used bulk to knock him over. Simon reached again for the gun, but his assailant recovered quickly and grabbed the pistol a split-second before Simon could grasp it. Simon looked up in just enough time to see the pistol aimed directly at him. He watched helplessly as the trigger was pulled.

The teen stood frozen with the gun extended for a moment, staring at the blood seeping onto the floor. Then with a glance at the direction of the pharmacist, he ran to the rear exit, knocking some medications off a rack in the process.

The pharmacist cautiously edged around the counter and watched the rear door to the alley swing shut. He took one glance at the customer lying on the floor, and ran back to the telephone. He dialed 911, and before the person answering could even speak, he was saying, "There's an emergency . . . I need the police and an ambulance!"

ONE

MARGARET BURST THROUGH THE BEDROOM DOOR and dove head-first onto her bed. She landed just as the door rebounded from the wall to shut again with a bang. Margaret kicked off her sandals and crossed her feet in the air above her, while placing her chin on her folded arms.

The San Diego sunshine streamed through the open window at an angle that suggested the time to be late afternoon. Pale blue curtains that matched the bedspread gently moved in the breeze. Both were slightly faded having been purchased at a second-hand store. Margaret had just completed a whirlwind of activity, unpacking the stack of gifts from her wedding and finding just the right spot for each item in their small home.

"What a job!" Margaret said aloud with an exaggerated sigh. *Won't Joe be surprised when he returns from work*, her thoughts continued. Joe had to return to work right away after the honeymoon, while Margaret had been able to take an extra three days of vacation. She leaned over to the nightstand and reached for a wedding picture placed there earlier that day.

First she studied her own reflection—brown hair the color of molasses (or mud, depending on her frame of mind), blue eyes, and a wide grin that showed most of her teeth. Margaret wanted the wedding pictures to look a little more dignified, but had a hard time controlling her natural exuberance. She had looked forward to her wedding day for as long as she could remember!

The dress was chosen with the skillful assistance of her mother and sister, attractively accentuating her smooth waistline and framing her face with its ruffled collar. Margaret's eyes shone with happiness, showing the same intensity as when they flashed with anger. Her nose was long, which tended to accentuate her thin figure, but put all together, she had a very pleasing appearance.

Joe repeatedly told her that she was the most beautiful woman he had ever known, but Margaret brushed aside the words as being mere flattery. She was unaware that Joe was drawn to the joy she took in life, which emanated from her very being.

Margaret was above average in height, but Joe still had a couple of inches on her. She felt that the photograph showed a pleasing contrast between her fair skin and Joe's darker coloring. Joe may have gotten his father's height, but his mother's Mexican heritage was evident in his overall appearance. Joe's deep-set eyes were a very dark brown, almost black. His dark bushy eyebrows could make him look quite fierce, but his generally pleasant demeanor softened the facial appearance to create a handsome effect.

A smile was on Joe's lips, but Margaret was aware that the photographer had caught what she called "the look" in his eyes, an expression that make it seem as though his thoughts were miles away. This look was familiar to Margaret and was one of the things that had drawn her to Joe. It was as though he had his own inner world. Margaret felt challenged to be the one person who would someday enter it.

Margaret got up from the bed and took the package of proofs of the wedding from the dresser top. She sat back down on the bed, cross-legged, and looked through them until she came to the picture of her parents standing next to the bride and groom. They were so proud of their daughter! If there was a mar on their wedding day, it was that there was no similar photograph with Joe's parents. They had both been killed in a car accident a few years previously. None of Joe's relatives came to the wedding because, as Joe explained, of the few there were, his mother's side were all in Mexico and his father's side were distant and scattered across the country.

Only a few friends and associates from the hotel where Joe was a manager attended the wedding. As a consequence, the size of the gathering was smaller than Margaret had always envisioned, causing her a slight measure of disappointment. She also settled for a September wedding when her heart had been set on a spring wedding. Joe didn't want to wait that long; a four month engagement was long enough for him. It hadn't been easy getting all the arrangements for the wedding made in such a short time.

"But the main thing is that I married a wonderful man!" she concluded as she put the pictures away.

Just then the telephone rang, startling her thoughts. Margaret went into the kitchen and picked up the receiver from the wall telephone.

"Hello?" she said, half expecting this to be one of the phone calls Joe was complaining about in which the caller hung up without speaking.

"Welcome back, Greta!" the voice on the line said enthusiastically, to Margaret's relief. Her previous room-mate called her by the pet name that Margaret's family used.

"Hi, Carol—I'm so glad you called!" Margaret replied.

"I hope I'm not calling too soon and disturbing your 'honeymoon feeling!'"

"No—Joe's not even here. He had to go back to work right away. I'm just putting away the wedding gifts. Would you believe that we got two identical crockpots and three Belgian waffle makers?"

"You might as well keep the extra waffle makers, so that when you have a table full of hungry kids you can crank them out real fast."

"We're not thinking about children yet, Carol!"

"That's just it—having children doesn't require a lot of thinking. Anyway, how was Hawaii?"

"It was fantastic! We had a great time except for it being a little too crowded for Joe. He said that he would like to vacation in a more secluded spot next time."

The two discussed the tourist attractions and lush scenery at length when their conversation was interrupted by a tone signaling another caller.

"I've got a call, Carol. We'll talk more about the honeymoon when you come over Wednesday to see the pictures."

Margaret hung up on Carol and connected with the other caller.

"Hello?" she said, with a pitch of excitement still in her voice.

"Am I speaking with Mrs. Bechmann?" a male voice asked.

"Yes, I am—I mean yes, you are—I'm Mrs. Bechmann!" Margaret was still not used to being referred to by her married name.

"I'm trying to track down a friend of mine," the voice continued, "and I came across this number for a Joseph Bechmann and thought it might be him."

Not knowing quite how to respond, Margaret replied, "He'll be home in about an hour. Would you like to try back then, Mr.—" she paused, waiting for him to supply a name.

"Can you just tell me where your husband is originally from, and then I won't need to bother him if I have the wrong person."

"Well," said Margaret slowly, "he grew up in Los Angeles, although I'm not exactly sure what neighborhood. I think he lived in two different places in the Los Angeles area. We just got married you see. . . ." Margaret felt a desire to explain that she had only known her husband for six months, but held back from discussing too many personal details with a stranger.

"In that case there's no need for me to call back later," the man replied. "I must have the wrong person. Thanks anyway."

Margaret hung up after wishing the man luck in his endeavor. She opened the refrigerator to begin dinner preparations. Suddenly she was struck by a thought that was faintly disturbing. Their number was unlisted. Where did the man find their number? Margaret determined to tell Joe about the phone call when he came home. In the meantime she had a more pressing puzzle. Where had she put the can opener?

TWO

JOE SAW THE EVENING HOTEL MANAGER enter the lobby and flashed a smile of recognition along with a greeting. Joe and Luis weren't exactly what he would call friends, but they respected each other and were on friendlier terms than many other hotel staff.

"How did everything go today?" Luis asked. "Did that crazy couple in 212 finally check out?"

"Yeah, they did," Joe replied with a grin, "but not before entertaining the customers in the restaurant this afternoon with a very loud discussion on 'Uncle Harry.' Apparently this uncle of theirs decided to write them out of his will, and they weren't too happy to find out after driving all the way from Spokane to visit him."

"What about their eleven suitcases?"

"I told them that tipping wasn't required, but they refused any help again. It took them over forty minutes to take the bags down one at a time on the elevator. Each time they went past the front desk, they had a *suggestion* to make, from new lamps in their room to a T.V. in the front lounge."

Every now and then certain patrons made the somewhat routine job of hotel manager more interesting. The strangest one was a man who held a three-way conversation with himself using different voices. After making some phone calls, Joe was able to track down a certain facility that was missing this particular resident. Fortunately, the man was glad to see the staff who came to escort him back, and cooperated with leaving.

Joe went over the day's operations with Luis, then bid him goodbye.

Joe's car was parked in back of the Mexican Royale hotel, an establishment which catered mainly to U.S. tourists desiring some Mexican atmosphere without having to cross the border, but also to Mexican businessmen who wanted to feel at home. Joe enjoyed his job which he had gotten due to his dual fluency in Spanish and English, rather than because of any background or experience in the hotel business.

The early autumn sun beat down on him and he paused to roll down the windows and let some hot air out before entering his five-year-old blue Buick. Joe turned on the air conditioner, then the radio, and began his drive home. It was a twenty minute drive in average traffic, while Margaret's drive was just a little shorter to the nursing home where she worked as a nurse.

The pleasant music coming through the radio mirrored Joe's thoughts. He still couldn't believe his good fortune in marrying Margaret. She was fun, and she was "classy," unlike the girls Joe had been interested in during his teen years. Most importantly, she loved him. It was Joe's certainty of that love that made him almost able to forget the feelings of fear and guilt which returned to him now only in occasional nightmares. For the first time in almost six years, he had been able to let go of the past. He had a good job, a beautiful wife, and the future looked much brighter than he ever thought possible.

Joe turned onto his street then pulled into the driveway of their small two bedroom house. Leaving the car parked in the street, he entered the front door. His spirits were unusually high, and he interrupted his whistling to call out, "Margaret, I'm home!"

"Hello, Joe!" she said as she walked out of the kitchen into the living room to embrace him. "I have some spaghetti sauce simmering—how about helping with the salad?"

"I'll do anything to be near such a gorgeous woman!" he replied after kissing her.

Joe followed his wife into the kitchen, a small area, but adequate for the two of them. He opened the refrigerator and took out some salad ingredients while Margaret located the cutting board and a couple of sharp knives.

"How did the unpacking go?" Joe asked, noticing for the first time that the boxes had been removed from around the house and new wall decorations had been added. A second viewing of his surroundings confirmed his growing suspicions that the boxes were not the only things missing. Several favorite posters and mementos from the Los Angeles Dodgers were nowhere in sight. He suddenly realized that Margaret had been telling him where things were now to be kept with a tone of voice that implied that he was supposed to remember it all. He drew a breath, but before he had the opportunity to bring up the subject of his missing "treasures," Margaret said, "I had an unusual phone call today."

"Oh yeah?" Joe paused, thinking of how to approach Margaret on the previous subject.

Margaret handed him a scrubbed carrot for him to cut up and continued, "A man called up, trying to track down a friend."

Joe suddenly tensed as a prickle of fear ran up his spine.

"He didn't leave his name, but he said that you were the wrong person."

Joe let out the breath that he was unconsciously holding, and hoped that his relief wasn't visible. As he relaxed his posture, his elbow bumped into the head of lettuce on the counter, knocking it to the floor.

"Are you trying to make *heads roll* around here?" Margaret joked as she bent over to retrieve the lettuce from under the table.

"Only when you forget who's boss!" Joe retorted, relieved to be changing the subject.

Joe and Margaret completed the salad, then sat down at the card table in the corner of the kitchen to enjoy the spaghetti dinner. Joe told Margaret the highlights of his day, then remembered to ask her for the whereabouts of his belongings.

"Don't worry, Joe, I didn't do anything to them. I just put them all in your closet."

"Which closet? My bedroom closet?"

Margaret smiled sweetly. "Well, I had time today to rearrange the closets, so I put all my clothes in the big closet in the bedroom since I have so much more than you do, and I put your clothes in the hall closet closest to the bedroom. I had to move some of your old stuff to make room for our wedding gifts, so I put your things in your closet and you can organize them later. I knew you wouldn't mind."

Joe did mind, however, and decided that he better set the matter straight right away.

"Margaret, I'm not sure that I want to have that closet for my clothes."

"Well, you could use the closet by the bathroom, but that wouldn't be very convenient because all the towels and linens are there," she replied.

Joe tried again. "Don't you have clothes that you could store somewhere that you're not using right now?"

Margaret gave him a puzzled look. "Why would I want to store my clothes when they all fit in my closet?" She changed the subject. "Carol called today and I invited her over for dinner on Wednesday."

Joe decided he would ask Carol for her advice. Margaret lived with Carol for the past sixteen months and could probably give him some ideas on the closet problem.

They cleared the table of dishes, then Joe dried while Margaret washed.

"How about taking me on in a game of chess?" Joe asked after the dishes were put away.

"That's too much thinking for me tonight," Margaret replied. "I'm a little worn out. What about that trivia game instead?"

Despite being tired, Margaret played better than usual and won the game after Joe's initial lead.

"I hope you weren't playing poorly just to let me win!" Margaret teased.

"I wasn't trying to let you win," Joe replied while leaning over and kissing her. "It's just that those beautiful blue eyes of yours kept distracting me."

"Do you want to play another game to have a chance at winning?"

"I was thinking of something else I'd rather do right now," Joe said as he stood up and pulled her into an embrace.

Margaret woke up with Joe's alarm the next morning and decided to make scrambled eggs and toast for breakfast. While they ate Margaret suddenly remembered the phone call from the day before.

"I forgot to tell you what was so unusual about that call I had."

"What about it, Margaret?"

"The man said that he came across the phone number for a Joseph Bechmann and I didn't remember about the number being unlisted until after I hung up. I can't figure out where he saw it."

Joe felt a surge of fear akin to panic. He nearly dropped the fork that held his bite of eggs. *I must stay calm!* he ordered himself as he tried to slow his rapidly beating heart.

Margaret was concentrating on putting jelly on her toast, or she might have noticed his sudden pallor and change in demeanor.

"That is strange," Joe said with a somewhat strained voice. "Did he ask anything specific about me?"

"No, as soon as I told him about you growing up in Los Angeles he stopped asking questions."

Joe's thoughts were tumbling around each other at a rapid pace. *What a fool I was to think I could start over! I'll have to be careful. I need to make plans—be prepared.*

Joe began to mentally review a "plan of action," one that he had thought often about but hoped he would never need.

Margaret was holding a one-sided conversation about her plans for a dinner party. Joe looked blankly at her for a couple of minutes before finding an appropriate comment to make. As they rose to clear the table, his thoughts turned to Margaret. For the first time a doubt arose within him. Would she—could she—give up the life of security that she believed they were living? He tried to push the doubt away, but it stubbornly lodged itself in his heart.

THREE

"YOU HAVE A VISITOR," the prison guard told Carl Milford, interrupting his work in the institution's food service.

Leaving the meat loaf preparation to another inmate, Carl followed the guard to the visitor's lounge.

"How's it going, buddy?" Rod Silvera asked as Carl entered the lounge. "Are they treating you well?"

Carl smiled back at Rod, but his pale grey eyes showed no warmth.

"It's all right," Carl replied unconvincingly.

His hair was in-between a dark blonde and a light brown, but in the florescent lighting it took on a grayish cast.

"How about you?"

Rod found it easier to talk about himself than to inquire further about prison life. Carl never had much of anything exciting to share as his daily routine seldom varied. Rod told Carl all about the RX-7 he recently purchased, feeling slightly guilty as he remembered that Carl wouldn't be driving for several more years. Carl listened politely for a while, then leaned forward to interrupt.

"Did you get the clipping of the engagement announcement I mailed you?"

Carl's eyes shone with intensity.

"Yeah, I was getting to that," Rod responded. "I think the 'Joseph Bechmann' in the announcement is our man."

"How do you know?"

Rod answered with some pride, "It wasn't too hard for me to figure out. I called information to find out if there was anyone listed by that name in the San Diego area."

"And?" Carl queried impatiently.

"There wasn't any number listed. So I looked up the girl's parents in the L.A. directory and they were listed. I said that I was an old friend of the groom's and had heard about the wedding. I said I had lost touch with him and wondered if I could get his phone number and address so I could contact him. I didn't even have to lie to get the information."

"And then what?" Carl's excitement was obvious.

"I wanted to talk to the woman, not to him, so that he wouldn't get suspicious. So I called a few times before the date of the wedding, but only José answered, at least I'm pretty sure it was him. I hung up on him without saying anything. They must have gone on a trip after the wedding, because I didn't get any answer for a few days. Finally I got the girlfriend—I mean wife. She said that he was from Los Angeles."

"When are you going to check things out?" Carl asked with keen interest.

"I thought maybe this weekend. I have a couple days off from work and I think I'll be able to take a drive down there."

Carl's smile looked more genuine, but Rod couldn't help but notice the menace that accompanied it. "Good. I'm looking forward to seeing him again. Let me know what happens."

Rod looked at his watch and said, "Sorry Carl, but I have to go. I've got a date tonight and I don't want to be late."

Carl replied, "Thanks for coming out. And let me know as soon as you can about José. I'll catch you later."

"Yeah, later."

Carl and Rod both stood up and were each escorted out of the meeting room, Carl to his job and Rod to the main door.

"What are you up to?" the guard asked Carl suspiciously, as they walked down the corridor.

"I'm going to repay someone what I owe, that's all," said Carl with a look of satisfaction.

Rod always had a feeling of relief when he left the prison after visiting Carl. He was aware of the fact that if events had been just slightly different, it could have been him behind bars.

Rod got into his black sports car and drove down the prison road to the highway. He was thinking about his drive to San Diego, and how he was going to make sure of this man being José, without being seen.

Rod was so intent in thought that he pulled out onto the highway without coming to a complete stop at the sign. He realized too late that a car was moving into his lane just as he pulled out. Rod heard the screech of tires and the sound of metal on metal as he felt the impact of the crash. His car veered off the shoulder and Rod felt his body bounce around in the car. Suddenly his head struck the windshield and he was aware of blood, then darkness.

FOUR

JOE WALKED UP TO THE ENTRANCE OF THE FIRST FEDERAL BANK, held the glass doors open for two elderly ladies on their way out, and entered the lobby. He had decided to go during his lunch hour, an idea shared by many other bank patrons, he noted wryly as he surveyed the lines of customers. He stepped into the shortest of the four lines and tried to subdue the impatience rising within him. The almost sterile surroundings did little to distract Joe as he slowly moved forward in line.

The teller was a middle-aged woman who was unsuccessfully trying to recapture her youthful looks. Even Joe's untrained eye could spot that her very blonde hair was artificially obtained. Purple corkscrew earrings dangled to her shoulders and vivid hues of make-up brought glances her way, but not with the admiration she imagined.

"Can I help you?" the teller asked, shuffling the checks and receipts from the previous customer into their proper receptacles.

"I want to close my savings account," Joe replied as he handed her the passbook to the joint account he had with Margaret.

The teller noted the balance of over eight thousand dollars and asked, "Would you rather we transfer the money into your checking account and you can disperse it from there, leaving your savings account open for future use?"

"No," Joe replied, shifting uneasily. "I want the account closed and the money in cash."

"Cash?" the teller inquired with obvious curiosity.

"Yes! Fifties if you don't mind!" Joe was irritated at the teller's inquisitiveness.

"Sir, I will need to see your driver's license or some other form of picture ID, and then I will have to get this withdrawal approved by a senior officer."

Joe handed the teller his license; she then compared his signature with the one on file and left to find the officer. While Joe waited, the irritation began to fade as nervousness crept in. Fear had been a constant companion in the last month since Margaret received that phone call. Joe hoped that by having the cash on hand and plans clearly made that he could sleep better at night. After all, this could be a false alarm. He wanted so much to return to the peace he had felt since Margaret agreed to marry him.

Joe tried to avoid thinking about what Margaret's reaction would be to leaving San Diego. He just hoped that if the circumstances arose he would find the right words to say. . . .

"Sir, I have your money for you." The blonde teller's voice interrupted his thoughts.

Joe breathed a sigh of relief and even managed a smile of thanks after she had counted out the money to him.

"Do you have anything for me to put the money in?" Joe asked as he realized that the money would never fit into his wallet.

"I'll see if I can find you an envelope," she replied.

The teller left her station and returned a few moments later with a small manila envelope.

Joe walked to his car feeling as though he held his whole future in that envelope. He would have to think of a safe place to keep the money, while making sure it was easily accessible.

"I might as well keep it in the car," he said to himself. "I might need to move fast."

FIVE

"JUST RELAX YOUR ARM while I take your blood pressure," said Margaret to the tiny gray-haired woman seated in front of her.

"What are you trying to do to me? You're hurting me! Help! Help!"

It was always the same with Georgina. She was ninety-two and confused.

"It's only a little pressure, Georgina. If you stay still, it will only take a moment," Margaret reassured her.

Margaret truly enjoyed her job as a nurse at the Cloud Ridge Care Center. She had worked there since getting her three year nursing degree, about eighteen months now. Her rapport with the residents was mainly a result of her own grandmother being in a nursing home. She knew how lonely her grandmother was at times, and how hard it was to be dependent in the most basic of tasks.

Margaret moved on to the next resident, also seated in the dayroom.

"Frank, I need to take your blood pressure!" she shouted into his better ear.

Frank had not understood her speech but was familiar with the routine and held out his arm to her.

Nancy Chang, another nurse at Cloud Ridge, walked past her carrying some charts. Nancy's parents owned a Chinese restaurant which Margaret was fond of.

"Heard anything more about our bonus checks?" Margaret asked.

Nancy paused mid-stride and replied, "Nothing more than that they should be here any day now. Orlanda said that Mr. Roster is still giving her an earful about how the union took advantage of the company."

Orlanda was the secretary and receptionist at the Cloud Ridge Care Center. She was successful in her job in part because she could listen to the complaints of the administrator on any number of subjects, and not feel it necessary to reply. An occasional understanding "hmm" or nod while she continued with her job duties was all it took to satisfy Harold Roster that his views had been adequately expressed and received.

The union representing the nursing staff had recently negotiated a small raise in pay as well as bonus checks for its members. This was cause for good spirits on the part of the staff, a more disagreeable than usual attitude in the administrator, and an extra measure of patience on Orlanda's part.

Tanya, the nursing supervisor, had heard this exchange and stepped out from her office behind the nursing station. She called Margaret and Nancy over to the station.

"I thought you'd like to know that the bonus checks are finally here."

As she expected, the announcement was met with enthusiasm.

"I'm going to hit the malls tonight!" exclaimed Nancy. "I've been looking forward to buying myself some new clothes. What about you two?"

"I'm not sure yet," replied Margaret slowly, "I guess I'll just put it in the bank. Joe worries that some disaster will happen, and wants us to have a lot of money put away in case it does. The only extravagant thing I've known him to go for was an expensive outfit for me while on our honeymoon. I'm still trying to figure out how to get him to agree to new living room furniture."

"But you did go to Hawaii," Nancy said. "How did you ever talk Joe into that?"

"My aunt and uncle gave us the plane tickets to Hawaii as a wedding gift. We stayed at the cheapest motel we could find, and Joe insisted that we eat at budget restaurants because the food is so expensive there."

"Just be glad you have a husband that thinks before he spends," said Tanya pointedly. "All our extra money gets spent on some expensive *toy* or hobby."

As Tanya spoke, she caught her reflection in a mirrored wall decoration. She leaned toward it, trying to pin her auburn curls back into place. Just then the administrator came around the corner and the three women busied themselves with various tasks.

Margaret entered the lobby of the First Federal Bank unaware that she was standing before the same teller who helped Joe two weeks previously. The bottle-blonde hair was the same, but the purple earrings had been exchanged for large diamond-shaped turquoise ones with black polka-dots.

Margaret had not been in the bank since her name was added to Joe's account. She did not need to handle any banking business as their bank was just a few blocks from Joe's work. But, as long as she had some extra time, she decided to take care of it along with some other errands after her 7:00 to 3:30 shift.

"I'd like to add this to my account. I don't have the passbook with me, but here is the account number."

Margaret handed the teller her bonus check and a piece of paper with the account number written on it. The teller entered the account number into the desktop computer, then glanced back at Margaret with a puzzled expression.

"Your account has been closed. All the money has been withdrawn."

Margaret looked up, startled. "You must have gotten the wrong account. We should have about 8,000 dollars in there."

"Wait a minute, now I remember!" exclaimed the teller. "I waited on the man who withdrew the money a couple of weeks ago. He wanted it in cash—all 50's."

The teller looked again at the computer screen. "Joseph Bechmann is the other name on the account. He provided us with proper identification. That *is* your husband isn't it?"

"It can't be," Margaret replied weakly. "There must be a mistake. My husband wouldn't do that without telling me."

The teller leaned forward with a look of condescending pity on her face. "It happens. You could always take legal action against him."

"No—I'll talk to him. There must be some reason for this."

Margaret grabbed her paycheck and the slip of paper, and whirled around to face the door. She bolted toward the exit, nearly knocking over a young child who was slow in getting out of her way.

Margaret drove back home in her Toyota Turcell, too upset to finish running her errands. She still had almost an hour to wait until Joe was to be back from work. She made the twenty minute trip home in fifteen minutes by departing from her usual style of cautious driving.

Margaret parked on the street in front of their home and walked up to the door. Her hands shook as she tried to get the key into the lock. This was so out of character for Joe. He was methodical and predictable. Why hadn't he talked with her about this?

She thought about calling him at work but decided against it. Personal phone calls were discouraged and this definitely was a personal matter. Margaret sat on the couch after turning on the television. A game show would have to suffice in keeping her mind occupied until she could ask Joe about their money.

Margaret stopped tracing the gold and green floral pattern on the sofa with her finger and sat up straight when she heard the familiar engine sound enter their single-car garage. She waited until the garage door closed with a small thud, then stood up to meet Joe. Joe entered through the door connecting the garage and the kitchen.

Without pausing to greet him she walked quickly over to him and said, "Joe, what happened to our money? I went to the bank today to put my bonus check into our account, and they told me that the account was closed."

Joe stood as if frozen and just looked at Margaret.

"Joe, is it true? Did you take out all our money? Why didn't you talk to me about it?"

Joe slowly set his keys down on the counter.

"Margaret, I had to. I've got the money in a safe place, but I can't tell you where it is."

"What do you mean you can't tell me where it is. What are you planning on doing with that money? I know that it's mostly your savings, but I am your wife!"

Joe moved a step closer to Margaret and she could see pain evident in his eyes. "You're my wife and I love you. But I can't tell you anything right now. You just have to trust me."

"Trust you! How can you expect me to trust you when you won't trust me with whatever reason you have for hiding 8,000 dollars!" Margaret's voice rose in anger. "What's going on?"

Joe reached for her forearm. "I'll tell you when the time is right. I need you to understand."

Margaret pulled her arm away. "The only thing that I understand is that you are keeping secrets from me, and I never thought you would do that!"

Margaret's words pierced Joe and he decided to share with her the burden he had been carrying.

"I want to tell you something else that you don't know about, Margaret."

"What do you mean, 'something else'?" Margaret demanded. "How many secrets are you keeping from me?"

"It's all related. I was hoping that you would never find out."

"You weren't even going to tell me about the money! What kind of fool do you take me for?"

Joe responded in frustration, instantly regretting his words, "I never thought you would act so childish about this!"

Margaret's eyes blazed and she took a deep breath, "If you think I'm the one being childish, then you better think again—and I'll give you some time to do just that!"

She grabbed her purse from the table and stormed out the front door.

"Wait a minute. Where are you going?" Joe called after her.

"That's my secret, and I'm not telling!"

Margaret ran down the driveway to where her car was parked in the street, got in, and slammed the car door shut behind her. The tires squealed as she lurched the car into gear. She randomly chose to head toward the downtown area, not looking back to see Joe watch her from the front door until she was out of sight. Tears were by now streaming down her face and she moaned out loud, "Now what do I do?" A thought came to her and she made up her mind. She took the familiar entrance onto the freeway and tried to get her tears to subside.

Joe walked back into the house and sat down on the couch. It was all wrong! How could they have argued like this? Where could Margaret have gone to? Should he have tried to follow? Frustration, doubt and fear swept through him. He tried to think clearly to make future plans, but everything eluded his logic.

SIX

IT WAS WELL PAST HIS USUAL DINNER HOUR and Rod was hungry. He exited off Interstate 5 at Oceanside and pulled into a drive-thru restaurant for a hamburger.

He missed his RX-7; it had been totaled in the accident. He had almost been "totaled" along with his car. Although his insurance company had given him replacement money with which he purchased a used Chevy Camaro, he was currently driving a beige Ford Tempo sedan. He needed something unobtrusive in order to accomplish his task.

"I'd like two burgers, a fry and chocolate shake," Rod said into the voicebox in response to a garbled, "Ow canne beov sarvice todayyy?"

"A burrger fryy and chocolate miilk, pleease moove farward."

Rod couldn't decide if it was microphone distortion causing the communication problem or if the user didn't speak English well. He took a deep breath and tried again.

"Two burgers, one french fry and one chocolate shake is what I ordered!" Rod pulled forward with the hope that somehow his order would be properly translated.

The young girl who handed him the bag of food was obviously not the person who took his order. She said, "Your order, sir" in perfect English, and she wasn't wearing a microphone. Rod drove out of the parking lot and took out a burger.

"Cheese—ugh!" He should have known that his order couldn't possibly have ended up right.

Rod got back onto Interstate 5 heading south. He had waited until evening to leave to avoid some of the traffic congestion along the coastal highway, but an accident was slowing things down considerably. He was getting tired and hoped he wouldn't have trouble finding a room for the night.

Rod originally planned on making this trip over a month ago, but a week-long stay in the hospital with a severe concussion and fractured ribs delayed things. Then it took a while to get things settled with his insurance company. His rates would be going up substantially, and he was just lucky not to get dropped altogether.

Rod had moments of regret in making his promise to Carl, but he had a debt to pay and this was the opportunity. "We were a team—we were tight. I'm not going to be a traitor like José!"

Rod was angry at José, but not like Carl was. Carl hated him. Rod couldn't quite understand the intensity of feeling that Carl expressed, but then he wasn't serving a prison sentence either, one that José would be sharing if not for Carl's silence and José's cowardice.

Rod finished his meal, vowing never to stop there again. He drove for a while with the radio for company, then turned it off to think through his plan. First he would find the house. Then he would wait and watch until he could make certain that this was his former classmate. All Rod needed to do was make sure, then let Carl know. Carl would take it from there.

After what seemed to be an eternally long drive, Rod took an exit into San Diego, then pulled over into a parking lot to take a look at his map. "Elm Street—here it is." Rod's finger pointed to the line on the map. He studied it to find the best route to take, then pulled out of the parking lot to head toward Helix Freeway.

Rod was mildly disappointed that the borrowed Tempo didn't squeal the way his Camaro would have. It didn't handle anywhere near as well, and he felt almost middle-aged driving such a "practical" car. He determined that he was never going to give up driving a sports car, no matter how old he got. Even if he got married or something. After all, he had an image to maintain.

Rod made it to Elm Street, but was several blocks away from the correct address. He swore in irritation when the road ended before he found the right home. He pulled over and took the map out again. Elm Street started up again a half-mile away. He just hoped he would find the house without further difficulty.

After making just one wrong turn, Rod found the neighborhood. He drove slowly along the road until he spotted the house number. He looked as long as he dared without drawing attention to himself, then drove a few blocks away and stopped to ponder his course of action.

It was dark outside, and the shades had been drawn. The garage door had been shut, so Rod wasn't able to tell if a car was there. But there were lights shining throughout the house, so Rod guessed that the occupants were at home. And at this time of night, most likely they were home for the evening. Even if someone were to go out, he wouldn't be able to recognize anyone in the dark.

Rod decided that the best thing to do would be to get a good night's rest at a motel, then get up early and watch the house. He would just have to follow them if they drove somewhere, until he could get a good look at them.

Rod drove around until he saw the INNexpensive. The sign was lit up to emphasize the "INN," with the unfortunate effect of also emphasizing the "expensive." One glance at the motel quickly corrected any wrong impressions, however. Rod could tell by its appearance that it was a budget motel which would serve his purpose for the night.

"I want a single," he said to the surly looking man behind the desk. The man wore a short-sleeved olive t-shirt that showed a tattoo with a snake on it.

"How many nights?"

"One, I think, but is it a problem if I need to stay another?"

"Nope. Room 23, and you need to pay in advance."

Rod hadn't really thought it would be much of a problem to stay an extra night. The motel had not kept up with the times and definitely was not AAA quality. He climbed the iron stairs to the second floor and settled into his room. He checked out the bathroom and the drawers. A Gideon Bible was in the bedside stand. It looked like it hadn't been touched for a while. Out of boredom he picked it up and began to page through it. He stopped when he saw the words:

"Do not avenge yourselves, dear friends, but leave room for divine retribution; for it is written, 'It is Mine to punish; I will pay them back, says the Lord.'"

Rod laughed at the irony of the words he just read and the task he was doing and threw the Bible down on the floor. "That's what I get for looking at it. I'll have to tell this to Carl. He needs something good for laughs to lighten him up a little."

He flicked the television set on in time to see a robbery take place on one of his favorite cop shows. He made a habit of jotting down innovative crimes and would fantasize about being the type of person who could outwit the police every time. This episode didn't have anything very interesting, however, and within a few minutes, Rod was asleep, still fully clothed.

SEVEN

ANNE BREWED HERSELF A CUP OF HERBAL TEA and made herself comfortable on the couch. She opened a book she had been wanting to read for a couple of weeks, but had been too busy. She was just beginning to recover from the move to Riverside on top of Margaret's wedding. This evening she could relax with the house to herself and read without any interruptions. Her husband Tony was league bowling tonight, her daughter Lori was at a friend's house and her son Jimmy was at a Boy Scout meeting.

Anne began reading the first chapter, but her thoughts kept drifting to her oldest child, Margaret. Anne hadn't heard from her in a couple weeks, and as mothers tend to do, she began to worry. Margaret wasn't very far away any more, with Riverside being a few hours closer to San Diego than Sacramento. But Margaret was now married and wouldn't be moving back home. Although Margaret had been gone over a year and a half now, Anne always hoped she would settle down closer to home.

Not that Riverside felt like home yet. Anne was born and raised in Sacramento and she preferred it over the Los Angeles area where she was now living. But Tony's company opened a branch office in Riverside, and Tony accepted a promotion requiring him to move there.

Even though the wedding seemed too hasty to Anne, she was pleased about Margaret's marriage; she really liked Joe. He seemed like a stable young man, unlike some of the others that Margaret had shown an interest in. He had managed to save enough money to purchase a home, an unusual feat for someone his age. Anne liked the attitude of respect that he showed toward her and Tony. The only time he had voiced disagreement with them was when they discussed a wedding announcement. He later apologized and said to go ahead and put one in the Los Angeles paper.

Anne attributed his reluctance for wedding publicity to his personality being somewhat reserved. She wanted Margaret to be happy, and hoped that Joe would be able to open up to his wife. It must have been awfully hard to lose both parents at the same time. Anne hoped that someday Joe would look on her and Tony as a second set of parents, but in the meantime she would accept things as they were.

Without even making a conscious decision, Anne slipped into her habit of praying for the people on her mind. She prayed that Margaret and Joe would have a strong and lasting love and that they would follow God's will and his ways. She could feel some of the anxiety lifting, and decided to give Margaret a call just to see how things were going.

Anne set her unread book down on the end table and walked into the kitchen to the phone, but before she could reach it she heard a quick knock on the back door and it swung open.

"Margaret! What are you doing here?" Anne saw the tear-stained face as Margaret wordlessly gave her mother a hug. "What's the matter—what happened?"

Margaret pulled away from her mother. "It's Joe," she managed to say before sobs erupted.

"What happened to Joe?" her mother asked fearing a tragedy.

"I just can't believe it, Mom!"

"Believe what? What happened??"

"He took all the money out and he won't tell me where he put it!"

Anne sighed with relief that it wasn't truly an emergency. "Sit down and tell me what happened," she said, leading Margaret over to the kitchen table. It was just like Margaret to blow things out of proportion. Things were either wonderful to her or awful.

"Oh mother, he doesn't love me, because if he loved me he would tell me what he's doing!"

"Greta, Joe would not have married you if he didn't love you. Now take a deep breath and tell me what happened from the beginning."

Margaret began to relate the story from getting the bonus check and putting it into the bank. When she got to her argument with Joe, however, she started sobbing again and her mother had to ask questions to piece the story together.

"Did he tell you he spent the money or that it wasn't your business what he did with it?"

"Well, no, he said that the money was in a safe place. But he wouldn't tell me where!"

"What exactly did he say about the money?"

"He told me he would tell me sometime, and that I would have to trust him."

"And do you? Trust him?"

At this question, Margaret stopped her sniffing and paused to think while she reached for a kleenex and blew her nose. "I guess I don't have any reason not to trust him. But I never thought he'd be keeping secrets from me. What should I do, Mom?"

Anne resisted the temptation to give her detailed advice and simply said, "Calm down, think about what happened, then talk things out with Joe. If you want to spend the night and go back in the morning, that's fine. But I think you should let him know where you are."

"I'm not ready to do that yet. I want to wash my face right now. I'll call him in a few minutes."

While Margaret was in the bathroom she heard her brother come in with a friend. "I'll just have to wait a while to call Joe," she decided. After putting her make-up carefully back on to disguise her tears she went into the kitchen where Jimmy and his friend were helping themselves to cookies and milk.

At fourteen, Jimmy was several years younger than her, but she had a special fondness for him, maybe because he was the baby of the family.

"Hi Jimmy, how's it going?"

Jimmy looked up and with a mouthful of cookies said, "Hi Greta, when did you come here?" He flashed her one of his special grins that endeared him to her heart.

"Just a little while ago. I think your name is Robert?" Margaret said turning to Jimmy's friend.

"Yeah, that's right. Rob Eller," he replied a little more clearly than Jimmy, having had a moment longer to swallow.

"I remember you from a couple visits ago," Margaret continued. "Where have you been tonight?"

"I would think the outfits would give you a clue," Jimmy teased opening his jacket to reveal his scout uniform.

Margaret had not noticed the uniforms with her concentration being on disguising her upset state of mind. Just then her dad walked in the kitchen door.

"Hi Jimmy, Hi Rob." Tony saw them first then noticed his daughter. "Well, Margaret, what are you doing here? Is Joe here too, or are you leaving your new husband alone already?" He put down his bowling ball case then gave his daughter a hug.

"I just felt like coming here for a little visit. I missed you is all!"

Margaret gave him a bright smile and hoped he wouldn't notice that anything was the matter. Usually it was her mother who was sensitive to the children's moods and she would inform her father when something was wrong.

"Well I'm glad you came for a visit. I missed you too. How long are you going to stay?"

Margaret felt a surge of panic. How long was she going to stay? When was she going to call Joe? What was she going to say when she did call? She made an instant decision. "I've got the day off tomorrow, so I'm going to spend the night."

"Well that's just great, honey. Let me just put away my bowling stuff and we can sit in the living room and talk. Where's your mother?"

Margaret had been wondering that herself. Before she could think of a reply her brother said, "Mom had to go pick up Lori. She's at Tina's house studying. They make it sound like they're doing schoolwork but I think they're really studying how to get Pete Reed and Eric Caggiano to take them to the school dance. I heard them talking yesterday, and they said—"

"That's enough, Jim," said his father, and by the tone of his voice he meant it. "You know you're not supposed to be listening in to their conversations."

"But Dad, it wasn't like it was a big secret or anything!" Jimmy managed to display a look of complete innocence.

"You know that it annoys your sister very much when you talk about her private conversations." Tony started to say more on the subject, but stopped himself as he remembered that Rob was present. "Rob, I think it's time for you to go home now, because if I remember right, Jimmy's still got some homework to do tonight."

Jimmy made a face as Rob said, "See you tomorrow, Jim," and walked out the kitchen door.

Jimmy hung up his jacket and reached for his homework as his father went upstairs. Margaret sat down at the kitchen table with Jimmy and kept him company until she heard her father come back down the stairs.

Margaret went into the living room and sat down on the couch. Her father took a seat in the chair across from her.

"It's too bad that Joe couldn't come with you. I suppose he has to work tomorrow."

"Yes he does," Margaret replied, thinking about how to avoid the subject of her husband.

"How are you two doing? Getting used to being married yet?"

Margaret was able to reply with some honesty, "Marriage is full of surprises. It does take some getting used to."

While Margaret was telling some of the things she and Joe had been doing recently, her mother and sister returned and sat down to talk as well. Lori was full of news about the friends she was making, and her involvement in joining the yearbook staff. Her mother gave Margaret a careful look and listened for a while before joining in the conversation. Margaret was relieved that her mother didn't say anything about the reason for her visit.

Margaret truly did miss her family, and talking with them helped put her current dilemma out of her mind. She was surprised, however, to discover that by the time her parents went up for bed it was almost midnight. She made her way to the guest bedroom, feeling guilty for not calling Joe. He was surely in bed by now. She would wait until morning to call.

The more she thought about their argument, however, the angrier she got. She lay in bed, turning their angry words over in her mind. "I don't know why I have to be the one to call," she fumed. "He must have figured out by now where I am."

Somewhere during the hazy time between being awake and being asleep, she decided that she wasn't going to be the first to apologize. She would simply be home when he returned from work tomorrow, and he would have to explain to her what was going on.

Although the decision seemed right to her at the time, it was one she was going to wish time and time again that she could do over.

EIGHT

ROD WOKE UP when the sun began to filter through the gap in the drapes. He sat up in bed with a start at the realization that he forgot to set his watch alarm.

"8:12—Oh no!" he groaned as he crawled out of bed and went into the bathroom.

Ten minutes later Rod was in the Tempo heading toward Elm Street. The evening before he noticed a small park area with a swing and a picnic table a half-block away from the house. He decided to park there and look like he was waiting for someone. He parked the sedan in front of the picnic area, then pulled out rolls and coffee purchased at a corner gas station. Rod also purchased the morning paper which he hoped would shield his face from anyone who might notice him.

The house appeared unchanged from the night before. Rod hoped he hadn't missed anyone leaving. After several minutes, Rod thought he caught some movement in the picture window out of the corner of his eye. Of course it was hard to be sure from this distance. He shifted positions in the car in order to be able to look more directly at the house.

Rod waited another twenty-five minutes or so and had just about decided that his imagination accounted for the movement he saw, when the garage door went up. He hoped that "the husband" was in the car. He watched as the car backed out of the driveway and was relieved to see that the driver looked to be male, although he couldn't be positive from this distance.

Rod started the engine and timed his departure so that he was about a block behind the Buick. He would follow the car until the driver reached his destination, and all he needed was one good look. Then his promise to Carl would be kept, and he could head back to L.A. to let Carl follow through with the information.

It wasn't easy following a car close enough not to lose it, but far enough away so as not to be noticed. Once Rod thought that he had lost the trail, but then the Buick reappeared from behind a truck that was hiding it from view.

Finally, the Buick slowed down and pulled into the back parking lot of a nice looking mid-sized hotel. Rod parked in the street along the curb near the entrance to the hotel. He watched as the occupant got out of the car. It was José. There was no doubt in Rod's mind. José had filled out and certainly looked different wearing a business suit, but it was him.

His task accomplished, Rod started to pull out into the traffic, but another car changed lanes right in front of him. He had to slam on the brakes to avoid hitting the car that had cut him off. He sure didn't need another accident! Rod glanced over to José who was just reaching the entrance. He wasn't looking in his direction, and Rod was relieved that his near-accident hadn't caused him to be noticed by José.

Rod headed toward the freeway, unaware that the squeal of tires had caused Joe to turn around. Joe did get a good look at the driver of the Ford. But as soon as he realized who the driver was, he determinedly turned to face the entrance of the hotel and walked with a casual stride without looking back for a second time.

NINE

JOE WALKED TO THE OFFICE behind the front desk of the Mexican Royale. It took all the self-control he had to nod greetings to Ray, the desk clerk, as though everything was fine. Fortunately, he was relieving Maria, and he doubted that he would have a problem making conversation. Maria talked enough for two people and wouldn't notice any lack of response on Joe's part.

"Hi Joe! Mr. Sanchez has already been here this morning and told me to tell you to make sure that the new maid does a good job in cleaning rooms today, because the last day she worked, which was Thursday, she didn't leave clean towels in several rooms, and one guy was really mad because he didn't realize that he didn't have a towel until he stepped out of the shower! That maid is a little slow—you know what I mean? And then, one of the waitresses quit last night, right on the spot with no warning or anything. They haven't been able to replace her yet so they're working shorthanded in the restaurant, and the other waitresses aren't too happy right now with this being a Saturday and all. Oh, and make sure that maintenance gets the leaky faucet in 311, because it looks like we're booked full tonight with the stunt car racing convention going on today."

Maria paused, waiting for a response from Joe.

"I'll make sure everything gets taken care of, Maria."

Satisfied that Joe heard all the important information she was passing on, Maria concluded with, "I guess that's all then, Joe. I'm going to go back home and get some rest, so if you have any problems today—don't call me! See ya kid!"

No one else would ever think of calling Joe "kid," but somehow Maria got away with things like that. Joe almost smiled as she gave a small wave of her hand and walked to the back exit.

It was a busy morning with a number of people still arriving for the convention. Somehow in the midst of handling all the various duties of the day, Joe tried to get his plans clear in his mind.

He still couldn't believe that Margaret would stay away all night and not call him. He didn't know if she was at Carol's apartment or her parent's house or somewhere else, but it was obvious that she didn't want to talk to him. He felt such pain when he thought of Margaret that he could hardly stand it. He wished that he could think of some way to convince her to come with him, but he felt after last night's argument that she wasn't ready to hear what he had to say. Besides, the time was short. Now that Rod had tracked him down, it would just be a matter of time before some authority or another showed up.

Margaret didn't need that hanging over her head and messing up her life. When Joe promised to love her in their wedding vows, he meant it. And leaving now, before she knew anything, could be the best thing for her. Later he would contact her and try to explain everything. Maybe she could even be persuaded to come with him. But for now, he would just have to leave her a message. He couldn't leave without letting her know how much he loved her.

Joe decided to take a late lunch break after things slowed down, and ask Ray to cover any problems for him while he was gone. Joe took a few minutes to write a note to Margaret and then sealed it into an envelope.

"I'm going out for lunch, Ray. If my wife Margaret should happen to stop by while I'm gone, give this to her."

Ray wondered about the contents of the envelope, but was too polite to ask. “Sure thing, Joe,” he said as he took the envelope from Joe and taped it behind the desktop. “See you later.”

Joe left the hotel with a mixture of determination and regret: determination to do the best thing for Margaret and steel himself against the pain of leaving her, and regret that Maria’s sleep would be interrupted when he didn’t return from lunch.

TEN

"DID YOU SLEEP WELL, HONEY?"

Margaret walked into the kitchen, still in her borrowed gown and robe and sat down at the table. Her mother was preparing pancake mix.

"Fine, Mom."

Anne noted the expression on her daughter's face and the curtness of her reply and decided that Margaret must not have slept very well at all.

"What did Joe say when you called him?"

"I didn't call."

"Don't you think he's worried about you, Greta?"

"Oh mother, if he was worried he would have called here. Besides, by the time I got out of the bathroom last night, Jimmy and Rob were here and then Dad came home, and I never got an opportunity. It was too late to call after you all kept me up talking!" Margaret glared at her mother accusingly.

Anne ignored her daughter's bad mood and calmly said, "You could try calling him now."

"Joe has already left for work and I don't want to talk about this when other people can hear him. I'll just go home and talk to him when he gets back from work."

Anne set aside the prepared batter and sat down next to her daughter.

"Margaret, I'm concerned about you. I'm also concerned about your relationship with your husband. Any marriage has obstacles that need to be overcome, and I want to see you and Joe work out the problem that you have."

"Mom, I don't need a lecture." Margaret said this rather unconvincingly as her lower lip began to tremble.

Anne reached to put her hand on top of Margaret's clenched fist. "Your father and I have had our share of struggles. You know we don't always agree on things and it takes time to work them out."

Margaret lifted her head at this point and shot her mother a questioning look.

"Just remember when we were discussing whether or not to move," her mother continued. "That must have taken us a couple of months to work out. I didn't want to be so far away from your grandmother. It could have gotten out of hand with each of us having our own very strong ideas on the subject, but we both made the commitment that our disagreement wouldn't get in the way of our love for each other. It wasn't easy, and we both had times when we were really angry at the other, but our love was the bottom line. Neither of us wanted to jeopardize that love, so we were each willing to give a little and come to a decision that both of us could go along with."

Although the threat of tears had subsided, a lump was still in Margaret's throat. "What would you do if you were me, Mom?"

"Pray and ask God to help you and Joe through this disagreement, then let Joe know that you love him and that you want to work things out." Anne answered without hesitation with years of experience guiding her advice. Anne reached over and gave her daughter a squeeze on the shoulders. "Your marriage deserves it."

Margaret sat for a moment in silence, then spoke.

"Mom, if you don't mind, I'm going to skip breakfast and go back right away. I need some time to think things through." She looked up at her mother with a small smile and added, "And time to pray. Say—can I borrow some clean underwear?"

ELEVEN

MARGARET CAME HOME to find the usual minor disarray that accompanied Joe's morning routine. The newspaper was on the table along with an empty cereal bowl and a half-empty cup of coffee. The bathrobe was in a heap in the corner of the bedroom along with dirty clothes from the night before, and the bed was unmade.

Margaret straightened the house, took a shower, and then dressed in the outfit that Joe picked out for her on their honeymoon. The bright floral pattern on the jumpsuit seemed out of season for the fall weather, but Margaret thought that it would bring back pleasant memories and soften Joe's mood.

Her mother's advice came back to Margaret, so she sat down on the couch with her Bible to pray. Margaret didn't intend to read her Bible, but its presence seemed to make her feel closer to God.

Margaret's family had gone to church as long as she could remember, but it was only recently that her parents were open in talking about their faith. Prayer was no longer reserved for a mealtime formality, and her parents would talk about Jesus in a personal way. This made Margaret uncomfortable at times, but she also had a respect for her parents in acting on their beliefs rather than just paying lip-service.

Margaret and Joe went to church together upon occasion since their engagement, but his Catholic background and her

Protestant background caused them to try various churches without making a commitment to any. Neither one had wanted to give up their religious upbringing. As a result, religion wasn't discussed much between them, as neither one wanted their differing views to disrupt their marriage.

Margaret folded her hands, and prayed a simple prayer asking God to help them work out their argument, then decided to read her Bible after all. She turned to the passage that was read at their wedding—the 13th chapter of 1 Corinthians: "Love is patient and kind; love is not jealous or boastful; it is not arrogant or rude. Love does not insist on its own way; it is not irritable or resentful; it does not rejoice at wrong, but rejoices in the right. Love bears all things, believes all things, hopes all things, endures all things."

The vows that she and Joe spoke at their wedding came back to Margaret. Even if Joe was being unfair, she shouldn't have stormed off to her parents' home. She would apologize to Joe for leaving him and not letting him know where she was. He just better tell her what was going on with the money!

The clock on the wall chimed 5:00. Joe should have been home a half-hour ago. She had just gotten up to start some chili, one of Joe's favorite meals, when the reminder of the time caused her to begin to worry. She did not want to talk to Joe on the telephone, but wanted to make sure that no problem had come up to keep him late.

Margaret dialed the number of the Mexican Royale, and was surprised that Maria answered the phone. She usually didn't work this time of day.

"Hi Maria, this is Margaret Bechmann, and I was just calling to find out if Joe left work yet."

Maria's answer plainly showed irritation.

"He most certainly did leave, and I am not at all happy about having to cover for him."

"What are you talking about?" Margaret asked, puzzled.

"You must not know any more than we do. He left at about 1:30 for lunch and never came back. Ray tried calling your home but didn't get an answer, so he called me up to come in and cover."

Maria's voice softened.

"You don't have any idea where he is or why he didn't come back to work?"

"I really don't."

Margaret's puzzlement had turned into fear. What if he had been in an accident?

"By the way, Joe did leave a note with Ray for you when he left for lunch."

"What does it say?"

"It's in a sealed envelope. Do you want me to open it up and read it to you?"

Margaret almost said yes, but considered the circumstances and thought better of it.

"No thanks, I think I'll just stop by and pick it up now."

Margaret hung up the phone and got in her car. It was hard to concentrate on driving, and the twenty minute drive seemed to stretch into quite a bit longer. At last she arrived at the hotel, and tried to compose herself. She entered and went to the front desk. She greeted Maria and Ray, and Ray handed her the envelope left by Joe. She opened the envelope right away, and noticed with irritation that Ray and Maria were still standing by her, waiting to find out the contents of the note.

She read the note and read it a second time.

Margaret looked up at the two employees, took a breath and said in a strained voice, "I don't think Joe will be back at work."

Ray looked at Maria, and Maria asked gently, "Should we consider it that Joe has given a resignation?"

"Yes," Margaret choked out.

"I'm really sorry," Maria said, sensing that Margaret was about to lose control.

Margaret turned and walked quickly to the exit.

Ray turned to Maria and said, "Joe didn't seem the type to walk out on his job—or his wife."

Maria just looked thoughtful and said, "You never really know what people will do. Just when you think you've got someone figured out, they surprise you."

Margaret was able to reach her car before the tears blinded her eyes. She read the note a third time.

Dear Margaret,
I'm sorry we had the argument, and I wish that I could explain everything to you. But I have to go away, and I won't be able to talk to you before I go. I wish I could bring you with me, but I can't. Try not to worry about me. Just remember that I love you and I'm doing what's best for you.

Joe

Margaret banged her fist on the dashboard, then crumpled the note into a ball. She started to roll the window down to throw the note away, but thought better of it. She stuffed it in her purse instead. As the realization of Joe leaving hit her, she put her head down on the steering wheel and sobbed.

PROLOGUE 2

Rose had just finished listening to the Funeral Director's instructions and was being escorted with her three sons to their seats in the front of the funeral parlor. She walked stiffly, concentrating on keeping her feet from stumbling as she felt everyone's eyes on her.

Andrew, her four year-old, paused to inspect a bulletin that had dropped on the aisle floor, but the oldest, Daniel, tugged him forward before Rose needed to intervene. The usher, a relation of her husband's, helped her and her sons seat themselves in the front row, squeezed her arm, and walked back down the aisle. He returned momentarily, escorting Simon's mother and sister who were seated to Rose's left, with the boys in between.

How was she ever going to raise these boys by herself? Rose gasped audibly at the thought and then choked back the tears that were threatening to break out. Her sons were watching her and knowing that they needed her to be strong helped her regain composure somewhat. For now she would block the crushing pain. She would cry later. She put her arm around Jonathon and Andrew as the rabbi began to speak.

"King David said in the 34th Psalm, 'The Lord is close to the brokenhearted and saves those who are crushed in spirit.'"

Rabbi Cahn was not orthodox and the funeral service reflected his individualized style. Rose and Simon had occasionally attended his synagogue and she was grateful that he could do the funeral.

"We are here today to grieve the loss of Simon Felder. There are many brokenhearted people here today who are stunned by this tragic accident, and I want you to know that the Lord Jehovah is close to you right now."

Rose wanted to laugh and knew that she was on the verge of hysteria. God wasn't anywhere near her or He never would have let Simon be taken away from her.

"Let us consider what kind of example Simon's life has left for us to follow," Rabbi Cahn continued. "He was a family man and was devoted to his wife, Rose, and three sons, Daniel, Jonathon and Andrew."

The pain that Rose felt began to recede somewhat as a different emotion struggled to emerge.

"Simon honored his mother, Helen, and sought to provide for her in her retirement years."

Hot and searing, this new emotion provided a barrier between Rose and the relentless waves of pain.

"Simon's sister, Hannah, will miss the older brother who has been a support and encouragement to her, especially during her recent struggle with cancer."

Three sobs escaped from Hannah's mouth before she stopped them with her hand. Simon's mother looked straight ahead as though not comprehending the reason for her being at her son's funeral.

"Simon's family and friends will remember him as someone who saw the good in life and shared this positive outlook through his sense of humor."

Rose's inner voice blocked out that of the rabbi's. *There is someone out there laughing all right—laughing that he has gotten away with this crime.*

The rage inside of Rose had grown in intensity so that it now consumed all of her other emotions.

The murderer is free, and my Simon is in a box!

Rose's thoughts were so vehement that she almost said them out loud. The realization had now come to her that she wanted revenge. She wanted a life for a life. She visualized facing the murderer and shooting him just the way he had shot her husband. But somehow the thought didn't give her enough satisfaction. He should have to suffer just as she was suffering—just as her sons were suffering.

The anger had now built to a raging fire. It would protect her from the hurt. It would drive her to continue living despite the grief that was making her want to run from life. It would enable her to get revenge—somehow. The anger would sustain her. God certainly couldn't.

TWELVE

CARL RE-READ THE LETTER FROM ROD. He skimmed over the unimportant parts, tired of hearing his complaints about the loss of his RX-7, and being bored with his job as a salesman in a music shop. Rod didn't know how good he had it.

> *You were right—José is in San Diego. I followed him from his house to a hotel—the Mexican Royale. He went in the back entrance so I think he works there. I can call the hotel and ask for sure if you think it's important. If you need me to find anything else out for you, let me know and I'll give it a try.*
>
> *After work tomorrow, I've got a date with Amy . . .*

Carl stopped reading at this point. He wasn't interested in hearing about Amy, either. So, José was living in San Diego. He found it hard to believe that José would work at a Mexican Hotel, however. José was never proud of his Mexican heritage, and had tried unsuccessfully to get his friends and family to call him "Joe." The name in the wedding announcement was "Joseph." José must be making sure that no one knew his given name.

It angered Carl that José was married. He shouldn't be married; José should be doing time just like Carl. Carl knew that when he got out, having a record would make it tough to pursue any romantic relationship. A job would be hard to come by. His life would never be the same. His only satisfaction was to imagine José finally getting what he deserved.

Carl still couldn't believe that José hadn't turned himself into the police. The murder was just as much José's fault as his own. Well, almost as much. After all, José was driving that evening, and it was José who goaded him into robbing the drugstore.

That's all it was supposed to be—just a robbery. José and Rod had been daring him to do it for a while. Carl finally agreed to it because he didn't want his buddies to think he was a coward. At the last minute, Rod backed out saying that he got the stomach flu. Carl always wondered if Rod had actually been sick, or if he was just scared.

Carl and José had stopped at a liquor store and Carl bought Tequila. Between the booze, a couple of joints and some pills they were really loaded. Carl still couldn't remember exactly how it happened. He never would be able to forget the man crumpling to the ground, however.

Carl fired the fatal shot, but the gun belonged to José's father. That was the link that Carl was hoping would connect José to the crime. And Carl knew where the gun was.

Carl eventually told his parents what really happened. That he wasn't alone, but that he had lied to protect José. He thought it would just be a matter of time before José heard about the trial and came forward to confess his part in the crime. Carl might have gotten a lighter sentence. Carl's parents wanted to hire a private detective to locate José, but Carl said no. He and José were friends, and José wouldn't let him down.

Carl thought bitterly about their friendship. When José moved to the neighborhood in fourth grade, it was Carl who came to his defense when a boy two grades older called José a "dirty spic." Without Carl's help, José would have been pummeled into oblivion in the fight that ensued.

Carl persuaded Rod to accept José into the "club" that they ran, and José enjoyed some status among his peers because of his association with them. The three of them remained close friends through high school, transforming the "club" into an unofficial gang. The members were expected to go to any lengths to help each other out. Who would have thought their friendship would end like this?

Now that Carl knew where José was, he was ready to talk to the lawyer his folks had hired. The lawyer hadn't been able to keep Carl out of prison, but with luck he could at least have José prosecuted as well.

Some days, Carl thought he would go crazy in prison. One thing kept him going, however. It kept his thoughts off of his dismal future.

Revenge sounded so good.

THIRTEEN

JOE WAS TIRED; the drive on Interstate 15 had been monotonously uneventful. He had driven straight through to Los Angeles, choosing to take the less direct route so that he wouldn't get stopped on Interstate 5 at the checkpoint for illegal immigrants. Although he didn't have to worry about his credentials as a U.S. citizen, he disliked the thought of dealing with any type of law officer.

As Joe drove near the Riverside area where Margaret's parents lived, he was strongly tempted to drive past the house to see if Margaret's car was there. Instead he headed west on Pomona Freeway toward downtown Los Angeles.

The resolve he felt so strongly about leaving Margaret behind weakened further when he pulled out his wallet to pay for some gas. His billfold contained a photograph from their engagement, showing the two of them facing each other with their hands clasped between them. The picture had given Joe a sense of security. It was a reminder that he now had someone to work for, to live for.

While viewing the picture this time, however, Joe experienced an aching loneliness so strong that it felt like physical pain. Marrying Margaret was the best thing to ever happen to him. Even though they had only been married two months, they were the best two months of his life. How would he ever be able to live without her, even for a while?

Although the area had changed since Joe had been there, he found a motel off the freeway just where he remembered it being. It was a small, single story motel with white stucco walls. It looked like it did six years ago, and most likely as it had forty years ago.

Joe got a room for the night, and brought in the small bag he had put in the trunk after the unusual phone call Margaret received. It contained only a few toiletry items and some documents, in addition to a change of clothing which was now wrinkled. He hung the clothes in the bathroom and turned on the shower, hoping that the steam would make the clothes a little more presentable.

Joe sat down on the chair next to the bed and removed the engagement picture from his wallet. He studied it and relived the day in his mind. . . .

After Joe had met Margaret that day by stopping to assist her with a flat tire, he somehow found the courage to ask her to go out for dessert. They hit it off right away, and after dating for several weeks, Joe knew that Margaret was the one for him. He baked a cake for Margaret's birthday, and brought it over to her. He made sure that Margaret got the piece carefully marked with an indentation in the frosting. When she took a forkful, she found a hard, shiny object.

"It's beautiful!" Margaret had squealed as she gave Joe a hug and a kiss and then went to wash off the engagement ring.

After calling her family with the news, Margaret and Joe had gone to a portrait studio and then out to dinner to celebrate.

Joe put the photo back into his wallet. Although it would be difficult to look at, the picture would also inspire him with hope that they would be together again.

Joe got up to turn off the shower, then decided to get something to eat. He drove a few blocks to a restaurant, and ordered a steak sandwich. As he ate, Joe's thoughts drifted to his family. In the six years since he left home, he hadn't once contacted his parents. Joe longed to call or write his mother to let her know that he was all right, but the barrier between him and his father kept him from doing even that.

Joe's father, Ernst, was a proud man who had survived difficult times to get a good education and become a hydraulic engineer. While growing up, Ernst's family had fallen under suspicion by the U.S. government during World War II. The FBI investigated his parents because of his uncle being a high-ranking Nazi officer. When the word got out, Ernst's father lost his job.

The strain eventually drove his parents to divorce, and Ernst was forced to help support his mother and sisters at an early age. His experiences drove him to be a success in school and work. But along with his strength and determination came a stubbornness and a coldness which to Joe, overshadowed everything else.

Joe's mother, on the other hand, was a warm and demonstrative person. She had no difficulty expressing her emotions, and Joe never doubted the certainty of her love. How she could love his father was a mystery to Joe. Joe couldn't remember exactly when he stopped loving his father, but there had been a point at which he decided that love was reciprocal, and if his father didn't love him, he wouldn't love his father either.

His parents were so unlike, that Joe wondered how they ever decided to marry. At the time, Joe's father was hired as a consultant by the Mexican government to help plan the irrigation system for the Colorado River diversion. He worked closely with a Mexican engineer, and was invited to stay at his home in Mexicali. That engineer eventually became Joe's maternal grandfather, as a courtship and marriage took place between his daughter Isabela and the young U.S. consultant.

After eating his meal, Joe knew he couldn't put it off any more. He had to see the house where he grew up, no matter what he would find. He might not ever have the opportunity to see it again.

Margaret had never questioned him much about his parents when he told her that they were both dead. They might be, for all he knew. The thought that they might have moved was also unsettling to Joe. What if at some point he decided to contact them and wasn't able to?

His brothers, Manuel and Fransesco were of college age now, and no doubt his father would have them enrolled whether or not they wanted to. Of course, they never minded being told what to do as much as he did. Elena would be in high school. Next to his mother, Joe missed Elena the most. She had lavished affection on the older brother whom she looked up to with such adoration. Joe wondered if his family still missed him; if they still talked about him.

Joe paid his bill, then drove the short distance to Monterey Park. The neighborhood was a fairly nice one, close to downtown Los Angeles. A few landmarks had changed, but the streets were the same. It surprised him that things had been altered so little. His parent's house was located where two roads joined together to make a *T*. Joe pulled over on the adjoining road to his parent's street, so that he was facing their house. He parked so that a palm tree partially hid his vehicle from view.

The house was a single story four-bedroom home with an attached double garage. The vine-covered brick and iron fence hid most of the front of the house, and Joe did not recognize the car in the driveway. It was already dark and Joe hoped that he would be able to see well enough by the streetlight to recognize anyone who might be coming from or going to the house.

He didn't have to wait long before a man parked a car in front of the house and got out. With a shock, Joe realized that it was his brother Manuel. Manuel's previously thin frame now looked muscular and he had grown several inches, but Joe had gotten a good look at his face and was certain it was him.

Manuel walked into the house and shut the door behind him. Joe waited for another half-hour, but all he saw were glimpses of shadows from behind the drapes. Disappointed, Joe finally decided to leave. He didn't want any neighbors to get suspicious of him and call the police.

As Joe drove back to his hotel room, he thought about the last argument he had with his father. His father was angry that his .45 was missing and blamed Joe for its disappearance. That his father's assumption was correct didn't make the accusation any easier to take.

"I knew you were no good!" yelled his father. "You take up with the wrong people and you never listen to what I say! And now stealing from your own father. Manuel and Fransesco would never do such a thing. What did you take it for, anyway? If you plan on being involved in criminal activity, you have no home here. Do you hear me? You might as well get out now."

Joe had heard his father, and would never forget the harshness of his words. His father had not listened to any reply, and when Joe's mother tried to intervene saying that he had no proof, his father banged his fist on the table and said, "I don't need any proof—I know my son."

Joe didn't leave right away, but he decided to leave after he turned eighteen. He just hoped that no one would connect him with the drugstore robbery before he had the chance to leave. He waited almost two months for his birthday, managing to avoid his father's wrath during that time. A few weeks after his birthday, he heard about Carl's arrest and left before anyone else awoke. He set his mind to the future and never allowed himself to look back.

Joe got back to his hotel room and decided not to watch any T.V. before sleeping. Having accomplished his goal of seeing his parents home one last time, he had a long drive ahead of him in the morning. It would take him several hours to get back down to San Diego depending on traffic, and then he would need to find someplace to leave his car before taking a bus south to cross the border. He hadn't been to Mexico in many years.

FOURTEEN

PHIL MEADE SLOWED HIS CAR as the Mexican border came into view. He and his wife Lisa had driven west from their home in Phoenix to Calexico. Mexicali was just across the border. His wife Lisa reached to rest her hand on his shoulder.

"Do you really think we're doing the right thing, Phil? How do you know it's going to be any different this time?"

Phil carefully considered the answer to his wife's question before replying.

"We're more prepared this time. We know how hard it's going to be. We're more familiar with the culture, and we know Spanish better. More than any other reason, though, I feel God's calling."

"But we thought we felt God's calling to the mission field before, and it ended in . . ." Lisa couldn't bring herself to finish.

"It wasn't failure," Phil said firmly. "We're coming back, aren't we? I think we rushed into things too quickly before. Maybe the Lord was trying to tell us to wait when Pastor Reed discouraged us from going. Our parents didn't want us to go then, either, but this time they are all supportive."

The couple was hoping to get across the border without being stopped, but a customs official noticed the small trailer they were pulling, and waved them aside.

Phil parked his car, and they both went into the building marked "Aduana," the customs office. They were prepared to part with some cash to avoid a lengthy delay. The line wasn't long, but the two men working behind the counter seemed to take forever.

"Tu pasaporte, por favor."

Lisa handed the clerk their passports as well as their birth certificates. The clerk looked the documents over, then began asking routine questions in Spanish, typing the answers on the tourist card. He used only his two index fingers to type with, and took his time in order to avoid making mistakes. Lisa began to get very impatient.

"Cuál es tu profesión?"

"Maestro," Phil answered, feeling relief when the clerk moved on to the next question.

Stating his profession as being a teacher was not exactly inaccurate as Phil would be teaching Bible studies.

After presenting the car title to obtain the car permit, the clerk stamped the papers and asked Phil to sign them.

"You may visit up to ninety days before your tourist card expires," the clerk said in Spanish as he handed the paper to Phil. "Everything is in order, you may go."

Phil and Lisa drove a short distance further until they saw the stop sign. A customs officer approached them and asked for their papers. He briefly looked them over, then glanced through the contents of their trailer. Considering the fact that they were returning to Mexico to live, they didn't have much other than clothing and a few household items. They wanted to avoid any difficulties such as paying taxes on large items or being questioned as to why they were being brought into the country.

"Go ahead!" the officer said, waving them through.

"Things are sure different this time," Phil said to Lisa.

He thought back to the first time they entered Mexico. . . . The clerk had asked suspiciously, "How long do you plan on staying in Mexico and what do you plan on doing while you are here?"

Phil had been warned that the Mexican government was cautious about letting people in who had no apparent source of income, and missionaries were especially unwelcome.

"Sir, we know that you are a busy man, and we hope to save you time by not going into details," Phil said as he lay a large bill on the counter.

The official's eyes had flicked to the bill, then he picked up the documents and pretended to study them.

After a moment he put them down and said, "Everything appears to be all right. Please sign here."

It had been hard for Lisa in particular to adjust to the idea of bribing officials. She knew that it was an accepted way for poorly paid employees to supplement their income, but it seemed so unethical to her.

Then, too, when Phil had purchased the Mexican auto insurance, the clerk took the bills handed to him without bothering to give Phil the change.

Phil remembered Lisa's anger erupting before they even got to the car.

"I hate it! The Mexican government is so corrupt!"

Phil's lecture on the positive changes being made in Mexico, and not judging other cultures by U.S. standards had only increased the resentment that Lisa felt. She didn't tell Phil any more about her frustrations in adapting to a new culture until they built up a wall between them.

Since leaving Mexico, Phil and Lisa went to a marriage seminar, and Phil learned to first listen to his wife, and then give advice afterward. He hoped that as he and Lisa learned to work together better as partners in marriage, they would also be better partners in ministry.

"It sure was easier than I expected," Lisa said, interrupting Phil's reflections. "Maybe everything will be easier this time."

Phil glanced over at her, relieved to hear her response.

After a few moments of silence, Lisa said softly, "I guess it's a matter of faith and trust, isn't it? If we believe that God wants us in Mexico, then it doesn't matter what the outcome is. We have to trust that God will work even if things don't turn out exactly the way we want them to."

She reached over to hold his hand. "If you're sure of our calling, I'm sure."

Phil gave her hand a squeeze and felt a large burden lift from his shoulders.

FIFTEEN

"OH, HI CAROL."

It was three weeks since Joe disappeared, and Margaret had been avoiding telling her family and friends. When Margaret's family asked why she came alone for Thanksgiving, she lied and told them that Joe had to work at the last minute to cover for someone else who didn't show up. She knew that the excuse wouldn't work a second time with Christmas quickly approaching, and Carol knew her too well to be put off for long.

Margaret wanted to wait before telling anyone, harboring the hope that Joe might show up soon. If nothing else, it would be better if she had something more specific to tell, about why Joe left and where he might be. She would just have to tell Carol that she was too busy to talk right now.

"It's been awhile since I've called so I thought I would check and see how you two 'love birds' are doing." Carol continued, "How's everything going?"

"Oh, just fine." Margaret had a hard time trying to sound convincing. "Say, I'm kind of busy right now—"

"That's O.K., I wasn't going to talk long anyhow. I just wanted to see if you and Joe could come over Friday night. I'm having a few friends over and I thought you might like to meet someone I've started dating."

Margaret didn't know how she could decline gracefully without telling an outright lie, and she knew she would feel uncomfortable coming by herself. Needing some time to think of a reply, Margaret stalled.

"Who is it . . . who are you dating?"

"His name is Paul, and I met him at a single's group at church. He's studying oceanography and he's tall, dark, and handsome like Joe."

"That sounds nice. I'm happy for you." As she said 'happy,' Margaret's voice began to quiver.

"What's the matter, Greta? What's going on?" Concern showed in Carol's voice.

"I can't talk about it, at least not yet. But I can't come to your party. I'm sorry."

"Are you and Joe having problems? Is there anything I can do to help?" Carol queried.

Margaret had a hard time keeping her voice steady. "I wish there was something you could do, but there isn't. I can't even think of anything to do about it."

"You know, Greta, if it's a problem between you and Joe I could have you talk to my pastor. He's really easy to talk to and he's had training in counseling."

Margaret decided to confide in Carol. "No, I guess I'd rather talk to you than a pastor. Joe's gone. I don't know where he is. He left a note saying that he was doing what was best for me and that he couldn't explain why."

"You mean he took off without any warning? Without any hint of a problem?" Carol was shocked.

"Well, not exactly. We had an argument over money and I went home to my parents, and when I came back he was gone. He left the note for me at work. His car was found in a parking ramp and towed to a impound lot."

"Did the note say anything else?"

"He said that he wanted to bring me with him, but he couldn't. And he said he loved me. But if he really loved me he never would have left and put me through all this!"

Carol asked gently, "Do your parents know?"

"I haven't said anything to them yet, but my mother knew about our argument. She tried to ask questions when I went there for Thanksgiving, but I said that I couldn't talk to her yet. I think she's feeling hurt, but I just don't know how to tell them. They'll probably think it's my fault because I left Joe without telling him where I was going when I went home to them. But this is different! I can't believe he did this to me!"

"Did you say that Joe didn't know where you were when he left?"

"He should have been able to figure it out!" The anger was evident in Margaret's voice.

"Do you think you did the right thing in not telling him where you were?"

"I was going to!" Margaret replied hotly. "I just didn't get the opportunity. I knew everyone would side with him!"

Carol replied evenly, "I'm not siding with Joe, but it doesn't hurt to examine things from his perspective as well as your own. You said that you were arguing about money. Do you think that he's trying to run from financial responsibilities?"

"That's just it . . . I don't know! He took all our savings from our account, over $8,000, and wouldn't tell me what he did with it! All he would say is that I needed to trust him. How can I trust him when he won't confide in me? And what am I supposed to do now?"

Carol probed delicately, "If Joe took all your savings, are you going to be, well . . . all right financially?"

Margaret replied hesitantly, "I've got my job, but the house payments are going to be tough. I'm thinking of selling his car, but it's not worth a lot. And there's something else. There's a chance, although I'm not sure yet . . . that I might be pregnant."

SIXTEEN

CARL MILFORD WAS TIRED. He had lived for the day he would get his revenge, and now that opportunity had slipped from his grasp. José was gone. According to the hotel where he worked, he just walked out one day and never came back. The speculation on the part of an employee was that José's wife never knew a thing about it. Rod had found a couple employees willing to talk when he went back to the hotel. Rod knew from experience that given an opportunity and a disarming smile, most people will talk about almost anything.

With the main ambition in his life gone, Carl slumped into a depression. He had prided himself in being smarter than the other inmates and was set on proving it to himself and others by working the legal system to get José prosecuted. Now the realization descended on him that he was no better off than the other prisoners, and that he had years left before he could hope for parole. Years of being confined, of being told what to do, and of fearing for his life. Fights were frequent, and nobody's safety was guaranteed. The prime of his life was being wasted behind bars.

Carl knew he needed something to take the place of his previous "project," but nothing else appealed to him. Out of boredom, he decided to sign up for a volunteer to visit him. He didn't particularly want to "build the friendship" that was the goal of the program, but it was a way to pass time. He certainly had enough time to pass, especially on the week-ends when he didn't have work duty. It was Saturday morning, and week-ends seemed to stretch forever.

Rod was the only one of his friends who still visited him, and he hadn't been around for a month, ever since he told Carl the news about José . His parents tried to visit once a month, but they were so caught up with their careers and social circle that it seemed to Carl they found him to be a source of embarrassment. He wondered if his graduation picture was still on the mantel, or if it had been put away as an uncomfortable reminder of where their son was.

When business associates came over, he could imagine his mother answering questions about her child:

"Our son? He's doing fine. He's not pursuing an education right now. He's taking his time about deciding what he wants to do. . . . Yes, he lives in California, but he's several hours away. Would you care for more dessert?"

A counselor approached Carl's cell.

"I have the name of the person who is assigned to visit with you. His name is Robin Leary and he will visit with you at two this afternoon." The counselor paused for a response from Carl.

"That's fine. I haven't got anything better to do, and I'm not going anywhere."

Carl's sarcasm was evident and the counselor walked away with a sigh.

Robin. What a wimpy name for a guy. Maybe I can have some fun with him, Carl thought to himself, *and lead him on a little about some sordid past.*

Carl went to lunch thinking about how he could blow this "Robin character" away with phony details about his murder rap.

After lunch he read a while before going to the visitors' lounge. Two guards stood watch over the inmates and their guests. He sat down in a corner chair to wait, watching the other inmates visiting with their family and friends. He particularly noticed the inmates who were lucky enough to have more than one visitor.

He looked up to see his counselor escorting someone about Carl's age to the room. Carl did a double take. Robin Leary stood about six foot four and had a very muscular build. So much for being a wimp! Carl quickly revised his plans for their visit. Robin didn't look like the type of person he wanted to have get angry.

The counselor pointed Carl out, then left the room. Robin walked over and extended his hand to Carl.

"Hi, I'm Robin."

Carl stood up and shook Robin's hand. "Yeah, I figured that out."

Carl decided to soften the words with a small smile. "Have a seat," he said pointing to the chair he vacated.

Carl leaned against the wall and gave Robin a long look. "So you're a volunteer."

"Yeah, I am; it's for a class project. One of the requirements of the class is to spend some time in community service."

"How did you happen to pick a prison?" Carl asked.

"I'm thinking about going into crime and corrections. Law enforcement has always interested me."

"And you thought you'd take a look at the kind of scum you'll be putting away." Carl couldn't hold back the sarcasm any longer.

Robin looked uncomfortable. "I'm sorry, I didn't mean to offend you. I don't think you're scum and that's not why I signed up for the volunteer program."

"Then why did you?"

Carl had the upper hand, a feeling which he enjoyed.

"It's hard to explain," Robin paused, "but I think that if I'm going to be able to do a good job, I'm going to need to understand the people I'll be dealing with. I don't want to have the attitude that once a person makes a mistake he can't change."

"What makes you think a person can change?" Carl asked.

"I've seen people change. I've changed."

"How?" Carl asked, not because he wanted to know, but just to needle him a little.

"Do you really want to know?" Robin asked.

"Sure," said Carl out of boredom.

"Knowing Jesus can change people," Robin said.

Carl shot a surprised glance at Robin. He didn't seem the type to need religion.

"What did you ever do to need a change?" Maybe Robin's interest in crime was out of personal experience.

"It wasn't so much what I did," Robin replied. "It was the kind of person I was. I was only thinking about myself and my own problems. I didn't care about anyone else. It wasn't until I became a Christian that God helped me to be able to deal with my problems. Then He turned my focus off myself. My experience isn't as dramatic as some other people I know, but it's real. I'm a different person."

Carl looked at Robin and thought, *I'm going to have some fun with him after all.*

SEVENTEEN

La Paloma was an upscale hotel in the Baja Peninsula of Mexico. It was designed primarily to cater to the taste of Americans, preferably rich Americans. Located on the outskirts of Ensenada, La Paloma displayed traditional Spanish architecture in a carefully landscaped setting right off the Pacific Coast. Joe's hotel experience and good timing got him a job as assistant manager.

The former assistant manager quit right before a large group of U.S. tourists were arriving to spend their Thanksgiving holidays. Joe inquired about a job before the owners had the opportunity to advertise, and was hired on the spot. The pay actually wasn't bad considering how poor wages in Mexico could be. Joe's background was well-suited to supervising the hotel and restaurant, and he enjoyed the work. For now, that was all that mattered.

As usual, Joe tried not to think about Margaret as he arrived to work and began delegating duties to ensure smooth operation for the day. He directed Fernando to clean the glass doors, and Landy to put a fresh flower on each table in the restaurant. He asked Homero to check the pool area for any litter or debris from the day before.

Joe was aware of some resentment on the part of the other employees that their new supervisor was not a Mexican citizen, but he did his best to treat everyone fairly. That earned him a certain measure of respect.

Life moved at a slower pace in Baja California than in San Diego. In the eight weeks since Joe began working at La Paloma, he impressed his employers with his industriousness, and his popularity with U.S. tourists. Joe always made sure to make inquiries about their home states, which especially put the first-time visitors more at ease with traveling in a foreign country.

The accounting had been done haphazardly, and Joe was trying to get the books in order, and also have better business records kept. He put in several extra hours establishing a more efficient filing system.

"You keep working like this, José, and someday you'll own your own hotel!" Señor Martínez would say.

Joe didn't think that Señor Martínez and his partner believed his story about wanting to discover more of his Mexican heritage by working in Mexico, but they didn't seem to care. They didn't ask any personal questions to Joe's relief.

After making sure that the proper supplies had been delivered to the restaurant, Joe sat down in the small office just behind the hotel's front desk.

"Buenos días, José."

Joe looked up at the sound of the owner's voice.

"Buenos días, Señor Martínez," he responded.

"Is everything going well?"

"I don't expect there to be any problems today. The supplies came on time, everybody showed up for work, and the weather is supposed to be good all week."

Señor Martínez said with a smile, "I suppose I can thank you for everything but the sunshine." He continued, "You don't need to be staying so late each day. You get here early and don't take off time in the afternoon. It's not good to work too hard. Now that the Christmas season is over, it's going to be slower. Why don't you leave at lunch time today? I'll be here all day."

Joe didn't really want to leave work early. As soon as he stopped working his mind was filled with thoughts of Margaret, and the loneliness was more than he could bear at times.

"I was expecting to finish getting the records up to date today," Joe said, hoping to gracefully decline the offer.

"How are you going to 'see the country of your ancestors' as you put it, if you never do anything but work? Go on, I'll personally handle anything that comes up this afternoon."

This was the closest Señor Martínez ever came to questioning Joe for an explanation of his move to Mexico. Not wanting to press the issue, Joe agreed to take the afternoon off.

EIGHTEEN

AT THE SAME TIME THAT JOE DECIDED TO GO TO THE PARK, Margaret stepped out of her car to face her parents. She took a deep breath and exhaled it slowly to prepare herself for what was to come. She had not been home in two months. Margaret avoided her family at Christmas by telling her parents that she was scheduled to work.

Margaret's mother called three days previously, insisting on being told what was going on between her and Joe. Margaret knew that her silence was causing her mother a great deal of anxiety. Her father still didn't know about the argument, and Margaret's mother was firm that it was time to let him know if there were problems going on. Not wanting to discuss her situation over the phone, Margaret told her mother that she would come to visit Saturday, her next day off. Her mother reluctantly agreed to wait until then.

Margaret walked up the driveway to the back door and let herself in.

"Mom? Dad? I'm here!" she called when she didn't immediately see anyone.

"We're in the den," her father responded. "Come on in!"

Margaret walked to the den where she saw her parents working on paying some bills. Her dad pulled out a chair for her.

"Hi, honey," he said. "We're glad you could come for a visit. We've been feeling neglected."

"Sorry it's been so long. Where are Jimmy and Lori?" Margaret asked.

"Jimmy's out playing ball with some friends," her mother responded, "and Lori is shopping at the mall."

Her mother had been watching Margaret closely, and seemed to be waiting for Margaret to begin talking.

"How's your new job going, Dad?"

Margaret didn't want to plunge into anything too quickly.

"The new responsibilities take a little getting used to," her father replied, "but I'm liking it. I'm glad we moved—and I think your mother is too," he said with a smile in her direction. Then turning back to Margaret, he said, "Alone again, I see. Is Joe working today?"

"I need to tell you something," Margaret said, clenching her hands together in her lap. "Joe left me, and I don't know where he is."

Tony looked first at his daughter, then at his wife, then back to his daughter again as if not believing what he had heard.

Anne just looked steadily at her daughter and said, "Tell us what happened."

Margaret directed her opening comments to her father.

"The last time I was here, Joe and I had just had an argument—about money. Joe took all our savings out of the bank, an amount of over $8,000 and wouldn't tell me what he had done with it. I left to come here without telling him where I was going. He never came home that day. When I went back, there was a note for me at his work saying that he wished he could explain things to me, that he wished he could bring me with him but he couldn't, and that I should try not to worry about him."

"Is that all?" her mother gently asked.

"Just that he loved me and was trying to do what was best for me. What kind of love is that?"

Her father asked, "You don't have any idea why he withdrew the money or why he would leave so suddenly?"

Margaret shook her head, no.

"It almost sounds like he was in some kind of trouble," her father speculated. "Maybe he had gambling debts or was in trouble with the law."

"Joe would never gamble," Margaret said emphatically. "Joe was very careful about money and insisted that we save for the future. And he is the most law-abiding person I know. He got passed on the freeway because he would drive the speed limit when no one else does."

"Was he afraid of getting stopped by the police?" Tony persisted.

Margaret started to respond in the negative, then a thought occurred to her.

"He had nightmares twice, and when I asked him about them, he told me that he dreamed he was being chased by the police. I guess I never thought anything of it."

"How much do you know about Joe before he married you, Greta?" her father pointedly asked.

"He never really talked much about his family. With his parents dying so tragically, I never really pressed him for details."

Margaret's mother turned to Tony and said, "I wonder if the police can do anything if he left of his own free will?"

"They can't, I already checked," Margaret interjected. "Anyway, there's something else I need to tell you," Margaret said as her parents turned back to her. "I'm pregnant."

Her father looked stunned.

"Oh, Margaret!" said her mother, trying to take in the news.

"I don't know what I'm going to do yet," said Margaret, looking down to avoid their gaze. "I don't see how I could raise a child by myself."

"What options are you considering?" asked her mother carefully.

"I don't like the idea of giving a child up for adoption, and I don't want to be a single parent. I made an appointment at a clinic to discuss the alternative."

Margaret didn't say the word "abortion" because she didn't think her parents approved of the idea. Margaret herself didn't approve of abortions, but she never had envisioned herself being in such difficult circumstances.

"You can't get an abortion, Margaret!" her mother said firmly. Then, remembering that her daughter was an adult, she softened her tone. "Abortions are wrong; it's a baby you're talking about, not just a pregnancy."

Margaret's jaw set firmly. "I have to think of my future. I can't put my job in jeopardy. I could lose the house if I don't make payments."

Tony interrupted, "We'll help you out. We'll do everything we can for you."

"Don't you see that I don't want to have to rely on you?" Margaret said with a loud voice. "I want to be independent!"

Tony replied, "You have just told us some very shocking things. I don't know why you took so long in coming to us, but we want the best for you, and we don't want you to do something that you will later regret."

"I didn't talk to you sooner because I have been thinking things through," Margaret practically shouted. "I've got to do what's best for me?"

"What about us?" Tony said, his voice beginning to rise as well. "We're the grandparents. What about Joe? He's the father."

Anne interrupted. "I better check on the cinnamon rolls I made for Greta's visit. We can talk more after a bit."

"What's going on?" said Jimmy poking his head in the door.

"Nothing," said Margaret angrily.

“Would you please stay out of here for a little while, Jimmy?” said his mother. “Your father and I have to discuss something very important with Margaret.”

“Never mind. I think I’m going to go now,” said Margaret. “I’ve got some things to take care of. I’ll visit again another day.”

“You just got here,” her mother said. “You didn’t drive all the way up her just to spend a few minutes with us! The last time you visited was—”

“I really have to go,” said Margaret, interrupting her mother. “Goodbye everyone. I’ll talk to you next time Jimmy.”

Margaret left the house. She didn’t feel up to having her parents pressure her on the decisions she was making.

“What was that all about?” Jimmy asked.

“We’ll talk to you later,” answered his mother. “I’d still like you to leave for a few minutes so that your father and I can talk.”

“OK,” said Jimmy as he looked at both his parents then pulled the door shut behind him.

Anne reached over to Tony, and taking his hand said, “Before we talk about Greta, let’s pray for her.”

NINETEEN

"ARE YOU READY, LISA?"

Phil and Lisa were leaving their small apartment in Ensenada to spend the afternoon passing out gospel tracts and inviting people to come to a Bible study that evening. They had gotten some names of people to contact from their mission board, and they had begun a Bible study with the hope of eventually starting an evangelical church.

There were now eight families attending the weekly meetings, and one man in particular seemed to have some leadership abilities. Phil and Lisa hoped that if a church was formed, the finances could be found to send Carlos Guerrero to Bible School for pastoral training.

"Ready, Phil. Do you have the pamphlets?"

The afternoon seemed to be a good time to talk to people. Many businesses closed for an extended lunch, and employees would be shopping and taking care of other errands. Lisa and Phil walked out of their apartment toward the park at the end of town. It was a sunny day and the temperature was warmer than usual for January weather.

Phil would engage the people they met in conversation, while Lisa would hand them a tract. The pamphlet contained some Bible verses that spoke about the forgiveness of sins available to those who trust Jesus, and the address of the meeting place for the Bible study was stamped on the back.

They usually approached the Mexican citizens rather than the tourists because they hoped to talk with people who might be interested in coming to the Bible study on a regular basis.

Phil and Lisa found the Mexican people to be friendly, and curious about what they were passing out. Lisa was quite tall with bright red hair, and tended to attract a lot of attention. Phil and Lisa had to be careful, however, not to attract a crowd, as it was in violation of Mexican law for foreigners to hold open-air meetings.

The park had the usual array of street vendors selling everything from fruit to seafood. Lisa paused to buy some gum from a young girl, not old enough to be in school yet. The girl's mother saw the transaction and hurried over to show Lisa some jewelry and hairbands. It was hard for Lisa to turn the woman down, but she and Phil had to be cautious with money. Their financial support was not fully raised, and they had to make do on a very limited income by American standards.

While Phil was engaged in conversation with a young couple on a park bench, Lisa noticed a man a few feet from the gazebo who was feeding the birds. He was very tall for a Mexican, and Lisa wondered if his height ever made him feel self-conscious. He glanced up and saw her staring at him.

Feeling embarrassed, Lisa felt the need to correct a bad impression. She walked over to him and handed him a pamphlet.

"My husband and I are inviting people we meet to attend a Bible study this evening," Lisa said in Spanish.

"Where is the meeting to be held?" Joe responded in English.

Somewhat surprised at his obviously American pronunciation, she answered, "Behind Romero's Auto Repair shop. It's only a short distance from here. The address is printed on this pamphlet. We begin at 8:00. Are you a tourist?"

Joe looked uncomfortable. "No. I'm American, but I work at La Paloma. It's a resort a couple of miles from here."

Lisa smiled and said, "Why don't you come if you have the evening free? It's always nice to talk with a fellow American."

Joe gave a cautious smile in return and said, "I just might. Thank you very much."

Lisa went over to rejoin Phil who was looking around for her. She glanced back to see the man leave the park and hoped he would come to the meeting. He seemed to her to be lonely. Maybe he was homesick.

After an hour of talking with people, Phil and Lisa returned to their apartment to eat. They were still on an American schedule for meals rather than a Mexican one, and ate supper earlier than other people did.

They went over the lesson for the evening, and Phil practiced reading it aloud in Spanish. His Spanish wasn't bad, but every now and then he would make some mistake that would cause smiles and occasional chuckles to break out.

Phil and Lisa walked over to the car repair shop which was now closed. The owners were finishing dinner in their living quarters adjoining the shop. They had very generously offered to have people meet in the enclosed yard behind the shop, saving the expense of renting a facility. If the weather was bad, the group would squeeze inside as best they could.

Phil and the shop owner began to set up benches made of bricks and boards, and Lisa entertained the owner's children while his wife cleaned up after the evening meal. People began to arrive, and noticing some newcomers, Phil went over to greet them.

Lisa looked up to see the man she had spoken with earlier in the day enter the shop and look around shyly. She went up to him with the children trailing behind.

"Hello, I'm so glad that you could make it," Lisa said, offering her hand to shake. "Let me introduce you to my husband."

She brought him outside to Phil who was still talking with the newcomers.

"Phil, I'd like you to meet someone, but I can't fully introduce him because I don't know his name. He's American."

"My name is Joe Bechmann," Joe said, shaking Phil's offered hand. "I work at La Paloma. It's a resort not far from here."

"I'm Phil Meade. We've been in Ensenada for about eight weeks. We're hoping to get a church established here."

"That's about how long I've been in Ensenada," Joe responded. "What a coincidence. Where are you from?"

"Phoenix, Arizona, although we went to school in Texas. What about you? Where are you from?"

Phil noticed Joe visibly tense.

"Southern California," Joe answered curtly.

Phil decided not to pursue the matter any further. "Well, I'm glad you could come tonight. I better get things started here."

Phil walked up to the front of the group which had gathered on the benches, then he and Lisa began to sing. After a few songs, they asked the group to join them in singing.

A few songs later, Phil put his guitar down and asked Carlos to pray before they began to study. Then Lisa passed out Spanish Bibles to those who didn't have one, and Phil began to teach about Jonah. He shared how Jonah tried to run from his responsibilities, and that God had to use drastic measures to get his attention.

Phil answered questions as best he could, sometimes asking Carlos to help. Carlos spoke English very well, and could sometimes take a concept that Phil was struggling to communicate and explain it in Spanish to the group. He was very gifted in using examples and illustrations that the people would understand.

When the lesson was over, Phil closed the meeting by praying that each one present would not run from God's calling for their lives. When he finished, he looked for Joe to invite him to come again, but he was gone.

TWENTY

IT WAS MONDAY MORNING, and time for Margaret's appointment at the FemCare Clinic. She had come home angry and tired from visiting her parents' home on Saturday. Margaret knew that her parents weren't to blame for her problems, but the person she felt to be responsible for her problems wasn't there, and her frustration was being taken out on anyone nearby. The week-end off from work hadn't improved her mood any. She was nauseated, and it was cold and rainy.

It was only a fifteen minute drive to the clinic, which relieved Margaret because she didn't want to have a lot of time to think about what she was contemplating. Being a nurse, she knew that the baby already had a beating heart, but she wanted to believe what her nursing instructor had said about the fetus not yet being fully human. Besides, she was just going to talk to the counselor. She hadn't made any final decision yet.

Margaret drove slowly along the street, searching for the address. In a pleasant-looking neighborhood, she found the office building where the clinic was located. The location was in a mostly residential area with a few office buildings and small businesses intermixed.

As Margaret parked in the street, she noticed a group of people coming around the corner of the block, walking on the sidewalk. Curious, she got out of the car to get a better look. She then saw that they were holding signs. *Protesters—those people are protesters!* she said to herself.

Margaret heard about protesters being at abortion clinics, but did not think that she would run into any. She stood still for a moment, then made the decision to keep her appointment.

As she drew near the entrance, a young woman came up to her and handed her a brochure.

"Please don't take your baby's life," the woman said. "If you need help, call the number in the brochure."

Margaret took the brochure, but didn't answer as she entered the clinic.

"I see you made it in OK," said the receptionist as Margaret came to the desk. "They showed up a half-hour ago. We've called the police about them, but the police haven't arrived yet. I hope they didn't bother you too much."

"No, they didn't bother me. My name is Margaret Bechmann, and I have an appointment for 9:30."

"Why don't you take this form to fill out. It will be just a few minutes."

The receptionist handed Margaret a form on a clipboard along with a pen. Margaret sat down in a corner of the waiting room. A young girl and her mother were quietly talking across from Margaret, and a women who seemed about Margaret's age was to her right. A young man was sitting next to the woman. They were holding hands, but not talking. The woman looked scared.

Margaret began to fill out the form. She had no difficulty with the basic questions, but had to ponder the more difficult ones.

REASON FOR APPOINTMENT?

Margaret wasn't sure what to put. She finally decided on: "To discuss options for a pregnancy that has come at a difficult time."

DOES YOUR INSURANCE COVER THE TERMINATION OF A PREGNANCY?

"Not sure," she wrote. She wondered how much it would cost if she had to pay for an abortion herself.

IS THERE ANY REASON THAT YOU SHOULD NOT UNDERGO A THERAPEUTIC ABORTION?

Margaret knew that the question was referring to her physical health, but she couldn't help thinking about what her mother said, that it was a baby, not just a pregnancy.

Her glance fell to the brochure handed to her outside the clinic. A picture of a baby at eight weeks gestation was on the cover. She opened the brochure and read:

"At only two months after conception, your baby can already respond to touch. Fingerprints are developed, and brain waves have been recorded as early as forty days."

Margaret folded the brochure back up and put it into her purse. She had read enough. She knew that she couldn't go through with an abortion and live with herself afterwards.

Margaret walked up to the desk and handed the woman the clipboard.

"I've decided to cancel my appointment," she said.

The receptionist looked narrowly at her.

"Did those protesters have anything to do with this?" she asked.

"They didn't force me to change my mind," Margaret replied. "Maybe they just caused me to think a little more clearly about what I already know is true. Thanks, anyway."

Margaret walked out of the front door and saw that the protesters were still there. She walked up to the young woman who had handed her the brochure.

"Thank you," Margaret said to her. "I don't know what I'm going to do about this baby yet, but I'm not going to get an abortion."

The woman gave her a big smile and said, "I'm so happy to hear that! Do you want to stay and talk for a few minutes?"

"No, I don't think I do," Margaret replied. "But I appreciate what you're doing."

"You're doing the right thing," the woman said as Margaret turned and walked to her car.

The drive home seemed to take forever. Margaret felt exhausted, and had a difficult time concentrating on the road. She got home and lay on her bed without even taking her jacket off.

Margaret felt relieved, yet scared. What would the future hold? She thought about her parents and how they would be glad to hear of her decision. Slowly her thoughts turned to God. Eventually she started talking out loud as she looked up to the ceiling.

"God . . . I'm scared. I don't know what to do. I want Joe back but I don't know where he is. I don't know how I'm going to make it financially. I don't know if I can raise a child by myself. I'm sorry for the mistakes I've made. Can you please help me?"

Then she added on the ending she had been taught as a child in Sunday school, "In Jesus' name, Amen."

With that, Margaret rolled over and fell into an exhausted sleep. She dreamed that strong arms were holding her and comforting her.

TWENTY-ONE

LISA WAS TIRED OF BEING INSIDE. It was the end of February, and the last two weeks had seen rain every day. The temperature was cold and the only interruption in the continual grey cloud cover was an occasional heavy cloudburst. Their small apartment was seeming even more cramped, and Lisa was feeling restless.

She was washing dishes that she had been too tired to do the night before. Lisa and Phil had invited a family of seven over for dinner the previous evening and it had been quite a task finding room for everyone to eat the meal. The three younger children had to sit on a blanket covering the floor, while the four adults and two teen-agers squeezed together at the small kitchen table. Although the visit was a welcome relief from the monotonous weather, Lisa was back to feeling down.

Even though Lisa and Phil had not been out to the parks to invite people recently, the weekly Bible study meetings had grown to ten families who regularly attended in addition to other visitors. The families decided to formally become a church, a decision that Phil was excited about. He knew that establishing a church was hard work, but felt that this time it wasn't all on his shoulders. The work would be shared by a number of people.

Carlos would soon be leaving for Bible School in Texas, where he would train for the pastorate. The school had promised to pay for the bulk of his tuition through scholarship money and a work study program. The future church would supply what they could toward the costs. Although they would miss him, Phil and Lisa's Spanish was becoming fluent to the point where they didn't need to rely so much on Carlos for translation.

"Lisa, I'm back!"

Phil had returned from helping Carlos make his travel plans and preparations.

"Hi honey. I'm almost done cleaning up after last night. How are things going with Carlos?" Lisa asked as she set down her dish towel and gave Phil a hug.

"He's a little nervous about going. He's not sure he has what it takes to make it through school. He'll probably need some special tutoring because he doesn't read very well. But I'm trying to convince him that with his natural ability in communication along with his strong desire to serve God, he'll do just fine."

Phil changed subjects.

"You know, it's starting to clear up and it looks like the sun is coming out. How would you like to go for a walk?"

"I'd love to. If I don't get out, I'm going to go crazy!"

Lisa grabbed an umbrella, just in case her husband's prediction was wrong.

"Let's go!" she said, taking his arm.

They walked down the steps from their apartment, and headed toward the business section out of habit.

"I'm glad we're back in Mexico," Phil said. "Things are going so much better this time, don't you think?"

"Everything but this rain. It's really getting me down. But you're right. Things are going a lot better, and I'm glad we came back also." Lisa paused then asked, "Why do you think things are so different this time? When we were here before, it seemed like everything was working against us. We didn't have the financial backing, we never got a group of people to be committed to starting a church, and then you got hepatitis. This time, everything seems to be going so much smoother."

"I've been thinking about that too, Lisa. This time we have more financial support. But what I think really makes a difference is that we have prayer support. We have five families back home committed to praying for us on a regular basis, and we know that they do a whole lot more than the usual 'bless the missionaries' routine. When we tell them the people and circumstances we want them to pray about, we know that they will follow through. Not only that, but we're praying a whole lot more ourselves. God can use us more effectively when we're more 'in tune' with Him."

"Phil, look!" Lisa interrupted, pointing. "Do you remember him? He came to a meeting several weeks ago. What was his name?"

"His first name was Joe, but I can't think of his last name. I think it started with a *B*, but I could be wrong," Phil replied.

"Let's go over and say hi," Lisa said. "He seemed like he could use a friend."

Joe had been making a purchase at an outdoor fruit stand, and was now heading in Phil and Lisa's direction.

Lisa spoke first. "Hello Joe. How are you doing?"

Joe looked up at them. "Doing fine," he said simply.

"Are you still working at that hotel?" Phil asked.

"Yes I am. I normally work Saturdays, but I took the day off today."

"You picked a good day to take off," said Lisa. "It's finally clearing up."

"Are you still having those meetings?" Joe asked more out of politeness than interest.

"We sure are," said Phil. "Wednesday evenings and Sunday mornings. You're always welcome to come. We're still holding them in the same place, although someday we'd like to have a real church building."

"You're planning to open a church, then?" Joe asked.

"That's our goal," Phil responded with enthusiasm. "The man who was helping me teach the Bible study is going to get training to become a pastor."

"You should come over to our apartment for a visit, sometime," Lisa said impulsively.

Joe hedged. "I'm pretty busy with my job. I don't have too much time for a social life."

Lisa noticed Joe's discomfort and said, "I understand. But if you ever have some time off, we want you to feel welcome to come to another meeting."

"Thank you for your invitation," Joe said. "I've got some things to do. . . ."

"Enjoy your day," Lisa said as Joe turned away and continued down the street.

Lisa and Phil walked the opposite direction.

"What do you think of him, Phil?" Lisa asked.

"He seems like a nice guy, but kind of the nervous type. He doesn't say too much."

"I still think he could use a friend," Lisa replied. "I hope he decides to come to another meeting. I'm thinking that he's one person we should pray for. It seems to me like he is carrying some kind of burden."

Phil looked at Lisa. "I didn't notice anything, but I'm not saying you're wrong. You do seem to have a special 'woman's intuition' sometimes."

Phil gave Lisa's hand a squeeze. "Tell you what. Since it's so nice today, let's get some food and we can have a picnic lunch."

"Good idea!" said Lisa. "I think it's time for a little celebration."

"Of what?" asked Phil, puzzled.

"Of sunshine and second chances."

TWENTY-TWO

AS IT TURNED OUT, Carl didn't have very much fun at Robin's expense. He found himself looking forward to the visits. Robin was close to his age, and he enjoyed talking about current events. Carl was used to feeling superior to those around him, but Robin was a deep thinker and could hold his own in a conversation. Carl's stories didn't shock Robin, and his needling didn't seem to irritate him.

It was another long Saturday. Carl tried to read a magazine in his cell, but he was bored with reading. Nothing seemed to interest him. He heard footsteps and saw a guard at his cell. Even a guard seemed a welcome relief from the boredom.

"You have a visitor," Leon Jackson said without looking directly at Carl.

"Yeah, who?"

"You can find out when you get to the lounge," Leon replied.

Leon Jackson was one guard who had an arrogant attitude toward all the inmates.

"Can't you just tell me who, for crying out loud? Who do you think you are, anyway?

"I'm not required to tell inmates the identity of their visitors," Leon said coolly.

Carl called him a name under his breath.

Leon said, "I didn't hear that, but I wish I had. I'd enjoy reporting you."

Carl contented himself with glaring at Leon.

"How's it going today, Carl?" Robin asked as he entered the lounge.

Carl sat down next to him.

"It's going. That's about all. There's a guard that's really getting on my nerves. Actually, a lot of things are really getting to me. I thought you weren't going to be able to make it today!"

"I got through studying earlier than I expected, so I decided to come out anyway."

"Well, I'm glad you did."

Robin was surprised at the honesty in Carl's expression.

"What do you like to read?" Carl blurted out. "I'm bored with everything."

"I've got just the thing for you," Robin said with a grin. He took out a small new testament from his pocket and tossed it into Carl's lap. "I got it for you. It's worth reading."

"A Bible," Carl sighed. "What's so interesting about reading a Bible?"

"It wouldn't be very interesting if it was just a bunch of rules to follow to be a good person," Robin said. "But it tells about Jesus and how to know him. Let me ask you something. You told me once that you're an atheist. Can being an atheist explain what purpose there is in life or how to be happy?"

Carl felt in the mood to talk. Even religion seemed tolerable as a topic of conversation at this point.

"No," he responded. "Being an atheist doesn't do anything for me. But it's the only thing that makes sense."

"Does it make sense?" Robin asked, leaning forward. "Do you really believe that human beings were made by accident? Or that when we die we turn into nothing?"

Honest feelings did not come easily for Carl, but for some reason he felt he could trust Robin. Maybe it was because Robin was so open with him.

"I wish I could believe in God," Carl said. "I wish I could be happy. But I don't think it's possible."

"Why not?" Robin asked.

"Even if there was a God, I couldn't be happy. I've done some pretty bad things. I'm not good enough."

"Let me read you something," Robin said.

He leaned over and took the new testament from Carl.

"This is a verse from the book of Romans: 'Very rarely will anyone die for a righteous man, though for a good man someone might possibly dare to die. But God demonstrates his own love for us in this: While we were still sinners, Christ died for us.' God knows the bad things that we do, and he loves us anyway."

Carl pondered that for a moment then asked, "What does it mean that 'Christ died for us?'"

"God is holy and there can't be any sin in his presence. I know this can be difficult to understand, but God required that a sacrifice be made for sin. Only Jesus could do it, because He was the only person not to sin, and the sacrifice had to be perfect. God takes the sin away from people who ask Him to, but it's only because Jesus made the sacrifice for the sin. Do you follow me?"

"I know people who go to church, and they aren't any different from me," Carl replied.

"Going to church is different from knowing Jesus. If you're trying to become a better person by going to church, the changes will be on the outside. But a relationship with Jesus changes you from the inside out. Once your heart is changed, then your life will change."

Genuinely puzzled, Carl asked, "How can you have a relationship with someone who's dead?"

"Jesus was more than a good person or a wise teacher," Robin replied. "He was God's son, and God made him come back to life after he was crucified to show us that death isn't the end—that there's life after death."

Carl tried to lighten the mood. "You should be a preacher, not a cop."

"We can talk more about it a different time if you like," Robin said.

Two days later, Carl witnessed a stabbing. Tension was always high behind the prison walls, threatening to erupt into violence. Fights occurred with very little provocation. This particular disagreement began over the choice of a television channel. Heated words soon became an exchange of blows, and suddenly Carl was aware of a knife in the hand of one of the two inmates. Before the guards could separate the two men, who were by then struggling on the floor, the one on the bottom got knifed in the chest. He later died.

Carl was sickened. It could have been him. He tried to avoid getting into fights, but it wasn't always possible. And death frightened him. Almost as bad as the "nothingness" which he imagined, was the thought that he didn't have anything to show for his life. His parents and his friends would remember him as a loser.

Carl was still feeling sour about the incident when Robin next came to visit. He repeatedly tried to bait Robin into an argument, and called him either "the reverend" or "preacher."

Robin, finally giving into his irritation said, "Do you want me to find someone else to visit? Remember, you're the one who signed up with the program!"

"OK, I'll lay off you," Carl responded. "You're a little on edge today."

"You're the one with the attitude problem," Robin shot back. "Don't take your bad week out on me." Carl was about to change the subject, but the frustration he felt at living a meaningless existence seemed to overpower him. He told Robin about the death of the inmate, and asked Robin if he was afraid of dying.

"Afraid? I guess there's some fear involved anytime you face something unknown. But if you think of death as being a transition from this world to the next, it's not so frightening. If you know Jesus, it's like being welcomed home."

Carl felt like someone with a terminal illness who was being offered hope for a cure. It seemed to him as though if he let this opportunity pass, he may never get another one.

Without fully understanding his reasons for doing so, he blurted out, "Can I try to know Jesus? I don't know how, but it can't hurt to try."

"Would you like me to pray for you?" Robin asked.

"Yeah, go ahead," Carl replied, not even minding that he was in a roomful of inmates, visitors and guards.

He watched Robin bow his head and clasp his hands together, then he did the same thing.

Speaking softly, Robin said "Dear Jesus, I want to pray right now for Carl. He wants to believe in you, and I pray that you would make yourself real to him. Amen."

Robin opened his eyes and was surprised to see Carl with his head bowed. He was even more surprised to hear the words that came out of Carl's mouth.

"Dear God, I do want to believe in you. I want you to take my sins away. Amen."

Although no more words formed on his lips, Carl felt as though God's presence was filling him and somehow communicating with him. It seemed as though a heavy load had been lifted from his shoulders. He felt good, better than any drug high he ever experienced. He opened his eyes and stifled the urge to laugh.

With his first genuine smile in years, Carl said to Robin, "He's real—there really is a God! I can tell he heard me. When I was a kid I tried praying a couple of times, but nothing happened. Something happened this time. Does God really answer prayer?"

Robin smiled back and said, "He just did."

PROLOGUE 3

"ARE YOU STILL WORKING ON THAT STOLEN CAR REPORT?

Disbelief showed in Officer Sam Wallin's voice. His junior partner's attention to detail was beginning to irritate him.

Just then the squad car radio squawked.

"Central—256, please respond to an alarm at Bob's Superette on the corner of Washington and Venice."

Officer Chad Raverez picked up the mike and replied, "256, 10-4, responding from Freeway 10 west of 110."

Sam turned on the lights and siren, then drove to the Superette as quickly as he was able to safely maneuver through L.A. traffic. Sam had been with the Los Angeles police department for almost twenty years, and had declined any promotion which would have removed him from the streets to a desk job. Sam hated office politics, and took pride in doing what he was best at: law enforcement and criminal investigation.

Things were different for Chad, Sam's junior partner. He had graduated six months previously from law enforcement school, and wanted to prove himself by moving as quickly as possible up the ranks. Chad was determined not to end up doing the same thing ten years later, much less twenty.

Just a few minutes later, the two officers arrived at the Superette. They were in time to see two young men, one holding a handgun, running out of the convenience store. The two suspects got into a maroon car parked in a corner of the parking lot, out of view from the store windows.

Chad yelled into the radio, "256, two suspects are fleeing the building and entering a Buick LaSabre! License Plate is out of view. One is wearing jeans and a white sweatshirt, and is armed with a handgun. Second suspect has on black pants and black shirt. Attempting to secure the situation!"

Sam had pulled into the parking lot and dropped Chad off at the entrance to the store. He wanted to ensure that if cornered, the men didn't go back in to take a hostage. Sam then positioned the police car to block the parking lot exit.

The LaSabre turned away from the police car and drove over the sidewalk and curb to get into the street. An elderly woman was walking on the sidewalk, but quickly moved out of the way when she heard the squeal of tires.

The LaSabre had to wait for a break in traffic, and just then a second squad car turned the corner into view. Sam pulled up right behind the Buick, while the second squad car stopped in front of it, boxing it in.

Realizing their predicament, the two men opened the car doors and ran in opposite directions.

"256, suspects fleeing on foot!" Sam told the dispatcher before opening the car door and crouching behind it.

The two officers in the other car did the same, while Chad pulled himself into the building entrance to be out of firing range.

"Stop and put down your weapon!" Sam shouted to the suspect nearest him.

The man kept running, so Sam began to chase him. Suddenly, the man pivoted and swung his gun hand toward Sam. Sam quickly dropped down, aimed, then fired his pistol. The man crumpled to the ground. Sam went over to disarm and handcuff him. He then went back to the squad car to radio for an ambulance.

Meanwhile, the other officers chased the second man to a chain-link fence. He tried to scale it, but couldn't do it in time. He was quickly surrounded by police.

"Freeze!" Chad yelled.

The man stopped dead-still and said something in Spanish.

"What did he say, Chad?" asked one of the officers.

"He surrenders."

Chad ordered him in Spanish to come down, where he was then frisked and handcuffed.

Chad brought the man to the police car and made him get in. Sam left the wounded suspect to the care of the other police officers and brought the first aid kit back to the car. The cashier stepped out of the store, and one of the officers went over to get a statement from her.

"It's a chest wound," Sam told Chad. "But I think he'll make it."

Chad called in that the suspects had been apprehended, one to be sent to the hospital under police surveillance and the other to be brought to the station. As Sam drove to the station, Chad said the Miranda Warning in Spanish. Chad couldn't help but notice the fear in the man's eyes. This wasn't a hardened criminal.

As Sam and Chad entered the downtown station with the suspect, they were given a message by a secretary.

"A 'Julie Harrison' called and said she wanted to talk with either one of you. She said that she had some information about a drugstore robbery that you two investigated a few months ago."

"Why don't you call her, Chad? I'll bring him to detention," Sam said, nodding toward the suspect.

Sam led the man away where he would have any property inventoried, then would be fingerprinted, photographed, and given prison clothes to wear after showering.

Chad was excited about the phone call. Maybe this was the opportunity to solve his first homicide case. He remembered the woman. She worked as a clerk in a pharmacy. A customer had been shot and died in the hospital without ever regaining consciousness.

No suspect had ever been found to match either the pharmacist's description or the fingerprints left behind. The weapon was never located. The clerk had left just prior to the shooting, and all she remembered was a van idling in the alley out back.

Chad took the woman's number from the secretary and used a desk phone to call her. She was home to answer the phone, and after being assured that he remembered her, she began.

"Today is my day off and I was driving to my mother's house for a visit—she lives alone, so I try to visit when I can—and I saw the van. At least I think it was the van."

Knowing that the clerk had previously been unable to describe the van because it was dark outside, Chad was disappointed.

"What makes you think that the van you saw was the one involved in the crime?" Chad asked, trying to show polite interest.

"The windows!" she answered excitedly. "I didn't remember the windows until I saw the van on the road."

"What was unusual about the windows?" asked Chad in puzzlement.

"They were shaped like guitars—electric guitars—with the necks pointing to the front of the van. And I got the license plate number!"

Chad thanked her for the information, and then traced the license plate number. He discovered that the current owner had purchased it just a week after the date of the robbery. A Carl Milford owned it previously, buying it a year earlier from its original owner.

Two hours later, Sam rang the doorbell at Carl's parents' house. Chad had to stand behind him because of Sam's large build.

Carl answered the door. He looked the black law officer up and down, then noticed Chad, who seemed dwarfed by Sam's size.

"What do you want?"

Sam took a step forward and showed him his identification.

"We're with the Los Angeles Police Department and we're here to ask a Mister Carl Milford some questions. Is that you?" Sam asked, noting that the young man standing before him matched the description on the driver's license check he had done.

Carl didn't answer right away, as if debating whether he could get away with hiding his identity.

"Yeah that's me," he finally said, not wanting to risk incriminating himself if he should get caught in lying.

Sam stepped back and looked at Chad, to give him the opportunity to begin with the questioning.

"We understand that you were the former owner of a 1984 custom built van," Chad stated for confirmation.

Carl visibly paled.

"What about it?" he asked with a hostile tone of voice.

"We have an eyewitness who states that your van was at the scene of a crime on November 6th of last year. A man was killed during the incident," Chad continued.

Trying to play it cool, Carl answered, "You must be mistaken. I'm sure my van was nowhere near a robbery."

The two cops looked at each other.

"What color van was seen there?" Carl asked, hoping that repainting his van prior to selling it would throw them off.

"It doesn't matter what color the van was then, or is now," Sam replied. "The custom-built windows are what our eyewitness remembers. It's easy enough to get a paint job done. You're going to come down to the station now to be part of a line-up."

"You can't do this—you don't know anything!" Carl shouted.

Sam ordered Carl into the back of the squad car, where he angrily got in. Chad radioed in that they were bringing in a suspect in an aggravated robbery and homicide case, to put into a line-up.

"Read him his rights, Chad," Sam said as he drove back to the station.

"You have the right to remain silent," Chad intoned. "Anything you say can and will be used against you in a court of law. You have the right to have an attorney present before any questioning, if you wish one. If you cannot afford to hire any attorney, one will be appointed to represent you. Having these rights in mind, do you wish to talk to me at this time?"

"Yeah! What makes you think I'm the one? You don't have any evidence! I don't even own a gun!"

Chad looked back at him and said, "You told us that your van was nowhere near a robbery."

"Yeah, so?"

"How did you know it was a robbery?"

Chad let that sink in for a moment, then continued.

"Also, how did you know that the weapon used was a gun?"

Three hours later, when Carl was chosen by the pharmacist in the line-up, he confessed.

TWENTY-THREE

THE SUN WAS HIDDEN FROM VIEW BY A HAZE, but Margaret knew that by mid-morning it would clear into a beautiful day. She wished she was able to enjoy the pleasant June weather, but her heart seemed to be permanently overcast.

Margaret sat in her parent's kitchen, drinking coffee and reading the Los Angeles Times. Margaret had been spending her week-ends off at her parent's home as of late. This particular Sunday morning she decided to stay home while her parents, Jimmy and Lori went to church. She just didn't feel like dealing with questions or wondering looks.

Being almost seven months pregnant, there no longer was a question in anyone's mind who saw her that Margaret was going to have a baby. Her thin figure hadn't been able to camouflage the fact for a while now. At least her appetite and energy had returned. Margaret just wished that happiness had returned as well.

Margaret still didn't know how she was going to manage. Her parents and Carol promised to help out, but the thought of raising a child alone was overwhelming. She decided against adoption as a possibility early on. Even if Joe never came back to her, she would have someone to love and live for—a reminder of the brief time that she and Joe enjoyed together before he left.

Margaret and her family discovered very little in their efforts to find out more about Joe. The police were not able to help. No criminal record was found on him. The Mexican Royale did not have any record of Joe having previous employment. The hotel did have Joe's prior address on record. The apartment management, however, no longer had his rental application, and couldn't provide any information other than how long he had lived there. Conversations with the hotel employees revealed only that Joe was well-liked, but was fairly quiet and did not talk much about himself.

All that Margaret had discussed with Joe about his background was that he grew up in Los Angeles, was an only child, and that his parents, Ernst and Isabela Bechmann died in a car accident. What troubled her a great deal was that she had been so trusting, and had not questioned Joe's vague description of his family any further. There were no previous records with the Pacific Bell telephone company of phone service provided under those names. Marriage, birth and death records in Los Angeles showed nothing. Margaret wondered how much Joe had been deceiving her.

Margaret had about given up hope of seeing Joe again. He would have contacted her by now if he intended to. Every now and then she would dream that Joe came home and life was good again. But when she awoke, reality would sink in. Even if Joe did return, Margaret doubted that she could ever trust him again.

When she and Joe married, Margaret felt as though she had found the perfect man of her dreams. She now realized that emotions had idealized their relationship. But despite her anger and hurt at his actions, she couldn't erase the memories of his good qualities. He treated others with courtesy and respect, and even their way of meeting was because of an act of kindness on his part. How could so much good and bad be mixed together?

The Los Angeles Times didn't have much of interest this morning. Margaret could tell by the headlines that they were searching for important news. She paged through the sections and was just about to put the paper down when a photograph caught her eye.

It was strange, but the expression on his face reminded her of Joe. A certain aloofness was there, and the dark bushy eyebrows gave him the same fierce look that Joe could have at times.

Margaret glanced at the article underneath the photograph, and was surprised to see that this man's last name was "Bechmann."

"What a strange coincidence!" she thought.

She read the article. The Los Angeles city council was honoring Frank Bechmann for his "innovative approach in creating water resources." His ideas were being implemented as "conservation measures for water use by the farming industry." He was from Los Angeles.

Margaret was intrigued. Maybe Joe had been lying about not having any relatives in Los Angeles. Maybe this man was a relative. He certainly had a resemblance to Joe, and the last name was the same.

Margaret set the paper down. She had already decided. It was an impulsive thing to do, but she would try calling this man to see if might be a relative of Joe's. He might get angry at being called on a Sunday morning, but she just had to know.

She dialed directory assistance.

"Do you have the number for a Frank Bechmann in Los Angeles?" she asked.

It always irritated Margaret when the operators didn't answer the question, but simply connected her to the recording. She got the number, then took a deep breath and dialed. A woman's voice answered.

"Hello?" The voice sounded polite.

"Hi. I'm wondering if I could speak with Frank Bechmann."

"He's not here right now. Who is calling please?"

"My name is Margaret Bechmann. I was just calling to find out if by any chance Mr. Bechmann is a relative of my husband's. Do you know if he might be related to a Joe Bechmann?"

There was a long pause at the other end of the line. Finally the woman spoke.

"Why do you want to know?"

Margaret hadn't expected this.

"Well—my husband told me that he grew up in Los Angeles. He's gone—he left, and I don't know where he is. I saw a picture of Mr. Bechmann in the paper, and they looked a lot alike. Not completely, because Joe has darker skin, but when I saw the name I wondered if they might be related."

As usual, Margaret had jumped into things without thinking through what she was going to say.

The woman on the other end answered slowly.

"We have a son named José, but we haven't heard from him in years. Some of his friends called him Joe. What does your husband look like?"

"Well . . . he's tall, over six feet, and he's got dark hair. I told you that his skin is dark. You see, his mother is Mexican." Margaret stopped as the realization hit her. "Are you Mexican?"

"I was born in Mexico."

"Is your name Isabela?"

"It is. What can you tell me about José?"

There was no mistaking the eagerness in her voice.

"Well, first of all, he told me that his parents were killed in a car accident and that he didn't have any close relatives."

"But you called here asking about relatives."

"I have reason to believe that Joe has been lying to me about his past. We haven't been married long and Joe left without an explanation. He took all our money with him."

"And you don't have any idea where he is?" Disappointment tinged Isabela's voice.

"I haven't heard from him in about seven months. I can't believe that he told me you were dead. Do you know why he left your home?"

"I—don't know for sure. I thought that maybe—well I really don't know."

Margaret thought that Isabela might be persuaded to share her speculation, given time.

"Would it be possible for me to meet with you and your husband sometime? I'd really like to hear about Joe, that is, José. Who knows, maybe we can come up with some idea as to where he might be."

"Yes, let's meet. Do you want to come to our house? Where do you live?"

"San Diego. But I'm at my parents' home right now not far from where you live."

"Would you be able to come tomorrow evening?" Isabela asked. "We have company coming over later today."

Disappointed that she couldn't come over right away, Margaret replied, "That would be fine. I work the day shift tomorrow, and if I leave right away after work I should be able to get there later in the evening."

Margaret hated the thought of driving back down to San Diego that evening, working a shift the next day, and then driving all the way up to Los Angeles and back. She considered calling in sick and staying at her parents house another night, but she didn't have any sick time left after going through several weeks of nausea.

Margaret got directions, then hung up. It was going to be hard to wait that long to meet Joe's parents. Excitement filled her, an emotion she had not felt since Joe's disappearance. She had forgotten to mention that she was expecting Joe's baby. They would learn that soon enough when they saw her tomorrow. She hoped that it would be a pleasant surprise for them.

TWENTY-FOUR

"CHECKMATE!"

Carl won the game of chess with Robin. Robin wasn't a bad player, but chess was Carl's game. He enjoyed working out strategy.

Robin put away the game board, and continued a previous topic of conversation.

"So tell me more about the other guy involved with the robbery."

"His name is José. He wasn't directly involved with the robbery, but he was the driver. And it was his dad's gun that we had. I covered for him in the trial. I said that I was alone that evening. But I always thought that he would come forward with the truth. He was only seventeen, and I was a legal adult, so he wouldn't have gotten a sentence like mine. But he ran, like a coward."

"What made you think that he would turn himself in when nobody knew that he was involved in the crime?" Robin asked.

"He owed it to me. You see, I saved his life once. We grew up in the same neighborhood. We did everything together. Anyway, three of us were on a camping trip with a summer youth program. The other guy is Rod, the one who visits me. We decided to sneak out after everyone else was asleep and go canoeing. The other two weren't experienced, and the life jackets were locked up, but we thought it would be fun. We got out to the middle of the lake and they decided to switch places. I tried to tell them not to, but they did anyway, and we capsized the canoe."

"And you couldn't see to make it to shore?" Robin asked.

"We had a full moon so we could see all right; the problem was that they couldn't swim. I never would have gone out there with them if I had known that. Anyway, they both panicked, but I managed to get them both over to the canoe. I didn't see any easy way of getting us all back into the canoe, so I told them to hang on while I towed them back. It was slow going and it took us quite awhile. Just about the time we reached shore, someone heard us, so the camp director was out looking for us with a flashlight. He was pretty mad, and almost sent us home the next morning. Rod and José both swore that if they ever had the opportunity to do something in return, they would. José's testimony might have gotten me a lighter sentence. I never intended to shoot anyone!"

Carl leaned back in his chair, the anger evident on his face.

"Did you ever hear from José at all?"

"Not once. He took off after I was arrested, but Rod tracked him down a few months ago. He must have figured out what we were doing, because he disappeared. Left his job and his wife."

"Why were you and Rod trying to find him?" Robin inquired.

Carl leaned forward and spoke in a low voice. "You see, I know where the gun is, and the gun is registered in his father's name. His fingerprints are all over it, and the bullets in it will match the one that killed the guy. I want José prosecuted for his part of the crime."

Carl stopped talking and started clenching and unclenching his fists.

Robin asked, "When you talk or think about José, what do you feel like inside?"

Carl glared at Robin. "What do you mean, what do I feel like? I hate him!"

Robin calmly probed further. "Remember that peace that you told me you felt when you prayed with me last time? What happens to that peace when you think about José?"

Carl lowered his eyes. "I don't know. It goes away, I guess."

"You can't be filled with God's peace and be filled with hate at the same time, Carl."

"I can't change the way I feel!"

"Do you remember that Bible verse I talked about last time? That Christ died for us even though we were sinful? When Jesus was charged with a crime he didn't commit and sentenced to death, he asked God to forgive the people that did it to him."

Robin paused, but Carl didn't say anything. He just looked at Robin intently.

Robin continued, "Jesus talked a lot about forgiveness. There's a verse in the book of Matthew, just after the Lord's prayer that says we need to forgive other people if we want God to forgive us. He also said that we need to love our enemies."

"How can you forgive and love someone who's an enemy?"

The anger was still evident in Carl's voice, but Robin recognized that it was an honest question.

"It might not happen right away. It's usually a process that takes time. But you have to remember that God loves that person just as much as he loves you. You have to be willing to trust that God will work things out for the best. That's a promise also, that God has the best interests in mind of the people who love him. The verse is Romans 8:28, and you can look it up when you get back to your cell."

Robin borrowed a scrap of paper and a pen from a woman visiting her brother. He wrote the reference down, then handed it to Carl.

"Have you ever had to forgive someone?" Carl asked.

Robin nodded slowly, then answered, "I have. I had a cousin that I was really close to when we were growing up. We were like brothers—maybe even closer. I don't know 'cause I never had a brother. Anyway, my cousin was killed by a drunk driver in a car crash. It completely tore me apart. It took me a long time to be able to forgive the guy who did it."

"How did you forgive him?"

"I had to. I was so angry about Scott's death that it interfered with my relationship with God. Every time I tried to pray, I felt like I just couldn't get through to Him. Finally I asked God to help me let go of my anger and forgive the other driver. I started praying for the guy, and after a while I realized what a load of guilt he must be carrying. And you know, I was only hurting myself with all that anger churning inside. It felt so good when I finally was free of the anger."

"And you think that I should forgive José." Carl's words were spoken as a statement rather than a question.

"I know you should," Robin replied. "It's not easy, but you have to if you want to have God's peace to stay in your life."

Carl spoke quietly, "I just don't know—I'll think about it. . . .

"Tell me about your family. What are they like?" Carl asked after a pause.

Carl found himself listening with interest as Robin described his parents and older sisters. Robin talked about some of the fun times they had together as a family. His sisters doted on him and took him along wherever they went. He and his dad shared an interest in baseball, and his mother taught him to play the piano. The affection with which Robin recalled various memories seemed entirely foreign to Carl's own experience.

"I can't believe they're all so good," Carl said. "Your mother must be trying for sainthood or something. You too—but I've never heard of a 'Saint Robin' before."

Robin wasn't sure if Carl was trying to be insulting or not. Before Robin could say anything, Carl continued talking.

"I'm sorry, I didn't mean to sound that way. I just can't help wishing that my family was a little more like yours. Maybe I would have turned out like you instead of wasting my life in jail."

"It's OK," Robin replied. "I guess I've had things pretty good most of my life."

"Tell you what, Robin," Carl said. "Would you mind writing down where that Bible verse that talks about forgiveness is for me after all? I think I want to take a look at it."

TWENTY-FIVE

"WHAT DO YOU THINK HIS PARENTS WILL BE LIKE?" Carol asked Margaret.

They were just entering the Los Angeles area.

"It's hard to say," Margaret responded. "I don't know anything about them. Joe's mother sounded nice enough over the telephone, but I'm sure that it will be hard to meet the wife of a son whom they haven't seen for years."

"Are you nervous?"

"Let's just say that I'm glad you could come along with me, Carol."

Carol had generously offered to come along and help with the driving as soon as Margaret told her the news. They lapsed into silence as Margaret concentrated on following the directions to the house.

"It looks like that's the house, Carol," Margaret said as she came to the *T* in the road. "Yes, that's the right house number."

"Wait a minute while I check in the mirror," Margaret said as Carol started to get out.

It was difficult to tell by the dome light how her hair and make-up looked.

After a minute Carol said, "You look fine, Margaret. Try not to be so nervous! Just be yourself and they'll like you."

"It's easy for you to say," Margaret responded. "You're blonde and beautiful and you're not carrying around a bowling ball."

"Haven't you heard about the pregnant woman's glow? Now go in there and shine!"

Carol followed Margaret up the driveway to the front door.

"I hope they don't mind that I came along," Carol said, suddenly sounding nervous also.

Margaret rang the bell and clasped her hands together in front of her. The door was opened by an attractive woman who appeared to be in her mid-forties. Margaret could definitely see a resemblance between Joe and his mother.

"Can I help you?" she asked with a puzzled expression.

"I'm Margaret, and this is a friend of mine, Carol Nicholson," Margaret said as she stepped forward. "I asked her to come with me."

Isabela's eyes strayed to Margaret's waistline and registered surprise. She caught herself staring and looked back up with a polite smile.

"Please come in."

"I didn't tell you over the phone, Mrs. Bechmann, but I'm expecting a baby," Margaret explained. "I got pregnant just before Joe left."

"You may call me Isabela," she replied, motioning them into the living room. "Does José know that you're going to have a baby?"

"No he doesn't. He left before I found out."

The man on the couch stood up as they entered the living room. Margaret recognized him to be Joe's father from the photograph. He neither said anything or offered his hand, but simply looked at the women.

"Ernst, this is Margaret," Isabela said as she moved to Margaret's side. She's expecting José's baby."

Ernst did not react to the news. He simply looked at Carol and asked, "And who is this?"

"This is Carol, a friend of Margaret's," Isabela replied.

Margaret moved forward and extended her hand to Ernst.

"Hello Mr. Bechmann. I'm very pleased to meet you."

He shook her hand then sat back down on the couch. Margaret and Carol sat down on a couch across from him, and Isabela seated herself in a rocking chair between the two couches.

"My wife tells me that you haven't seen my son in several months," Ernst began. "What were the circumstances under which he left?"

Margaret felt intimidated by Ernst's abruptness, but she determined to wait a while before deciding whether or not she liked him.

"Joe cleared out our savings account of several thousand dollars, and when I asked him where the money was he wouldn't tell me. We had an argument and I left to spend the night at my parents' house. I didn't tell him where I was going and when I came back the next day, he was gone. He left a note at his job saying that he had to go away and that he couldn't talk to me before he left. I haven't heard from him since."

"And you have no idea where he might be?"

Ernst questioned Margaret as though she was being interrogated for a crime. His blue eyes bore into her.

"I was actually hoping that you might have some idea. Until yesterday I had no idea you were still alive. Joe told me that you both were killed in a car accident. But I'm confused. Joe told me that your name was Ernst, and your wife calls you Ernst, but your name was printed as Frank in the newspaper article I read."

"My middle name is Franklin, and I go by Frank at work. It sounds more American." Ernst continued, "What can you tell me about my son?"

Margaret began to bristle at the phrase 'my son' and replied, "My husband had a job as a manager of the Mexican Royale hotel in San Diego. We have a house that Joe was able to purchase before we got married. He likes baseball and football, going for walks and—"

"Why did my son marry you?" Ernst interrupted.

Margaret's temper rose and she said with an angry voice, "He married me because he loved me and because I loved him. In the note that he left me he told me that he loved me. And I still love him!"

Carol reached over to put her hand on Margaret's shoulder and Isabela changed the subject.

"I have some photographs of José as a child and while growing up that I thought you might like to see."

Isabela stood up and took an envelope off of an end table and handed it to Margaret.

Margaret smiled at her and said, "Thank you very much. I also brought some photographs for you to look at. Some were taken before we were married, and some are from our wedding."

Margaret took the photographs out of her purse and handed them to Isabela.

"You've got other children?" Margaret asked Isabela in surprise as she studied the photographs.

"Yes, we have four children. Manuel is the next oldest after José, and Fransesco follows him. Elena is the youngest."

"Where are they now?" Margaret asked.

"Fransesco is away at college, and we asked Manuel and Elena to go out this evening so that we could talk to you alone first," Isabela responded.

Carol spoke for the first time. "Your children are all good-looking, Mr. and Mrs. Bechmann."

Margaret looked at Isabela and said, "When I spoke with you on the phone, you said that you had an idea as to why Joe left your home?"

Isabela shot a glance at Ernst who simply looked straight ahead with a fierce expression on his face.

"We don't know anything for sure, but he left just after his best friend was arrested in connection with a murder. It may be just a coincidence, because his friend said that he was alone when he committed the crime. But José was out that evening, and it's possible that he may have had some involvement with it. Ernst had a gun which disappeared that same day."

Margaret looked stunned. "A murder?"

"Apparently Carl, that's the name of José's friend, was intending on robbing a drugstore. But somehow he ended up shooting a customer who died shortly afterwards."

"Were there any witnesses?" Margaret asked. "Are you sure that Joe wasn't in the drugstore?"

"The pharmacist witnessed the crime. And he said that only Carl was in the store. So we don't know what to think."

"Did you have any thoughts on where he might have gone to when he left?" Margaret again spoke to Isabela and ignored Ernst.

"I always wondered if he decided to go to Mexico. We have relatives in Mexicali and we visited Mexico often when José was younger. As a matter of fact, Joe was born there. I was really nervous with my first pregnancy, and my sister's husband in Mexicali is a doctor. Anyway, I was wrong about José going to Mexico, wasn't I?"

Isabela smiled a sad smile at Margaret.

Margaret thought for a moment and said, "I wonder if he's there now. Aren't there a lot of resorts and hotels in Mexico?"

"Not so much in Mexicali, but in other cities where tourism is stronger," Isabela replied.

Carol looked at Margaret and asked, "Do you think he might have gone there and gotten a job as a manager of a hotel?"

"I don't have any better ideas. You know he speaks Spanish, don't you?" Margaret asked Carol.

"I never realized that," Carol responded. "I suppose that would be a good place to go if you could get a job."

Isabela resumed her role as hostess. "Can I get you both something to drink? Some tea or coffee?"

Margaret looked from her over to Joe's father who had settled back into the couch with his arms folded in front of him.

"No, thank you. I appreciate the offer, but I think that Carol and I better be heading back. We have a long drive ahead of us." Margaret stood up and continued, "I'd like to keep in touch if you don't mind. Especially with your grandchild on the way."

Carol rose also and said, "It was nice to meet you both."

Ernst remained seated while Isabela walked them to the door.

"I would like it very much if you would come and visit again," Isabela said to Margaret. "José's brothers and sister would like to meet you."

Isabela squeezed Margaret's arm, a gesture which Margaret appreciated. She was glad that at least Joe's mother was accepting of her.

"Good-bye," Margaret said warmly to Isabela, "and thank you very much. I'm looking forward to getting to know you."

TWENTY-SIX

JOE SAT DOWN ON THE BENCH IN THE PARK and watched the birds vie for the crumbs he was tossing to them. It was an early Sunday morning and he had nothing to do all day. His apartment required very little upkeep and he ate most of his meals at La Paloma. Joe dreaded his days off because all he had to do was think. And that was the last thing he wanted to do.

Not only was Joe incredibly lonely, he was beginning to think that facing a jail term was preferable to having fear hang over his life. He didn't know what was worse: dreaming of returning to Margaret and discovering that she didn't love him anymore or dreaming that he spent the rest of his life rotting in a prison cell. In any case the future was uncertain and that uncertainty was making him desperate.

Joe stood up and started pacing, scaring the birds away. His thoughts and emotions were in a turmoil. Something had to change. He couldn't continue living this way.

All at once a picture entered Joe's thoughts. The story he heard several months previously came back to him. He saw Jonah running for his life and thinking that he had finally found safety in buying passage on a ship. But the ship only brought him closer to danger, and he ended up inside a fish with no way out.

Joe resisted the impulse to shake his fist at the heavens. God was doing this to him. God was hunting him down, caging him in and leaving him with no options. He felt just as trapped as Jonah.

One thought persisted, however. Jonah called out to God, and God rescued him from certain death. Jonah wasn't freed to do whatever he wanted, however. Jonah had to do what God called him to do.

Joe sat back down on the bench. He leaned forward and put his head on his clasped hands. Did he have the same choice as Jonah: to continue running and face a sure death—which a lonely life without any meaning or purpose certainly was—or to call out to God for help and have to spend the rest of his life in servitude?

Joe stood up again. He felt the need to talk to someone so strongly that it was almost an unbearable pressure. He thought of the man who had taught the lesson on Jonah. Phil Meade seemed to be the kind of person he could trust. Joe looked at his watch. It read 8:15. It was probably a little early to try to call. Then the realization dawned on him that it was Sunday and that Phil would be leading a church service that morning. Phil had mentioned the starting time as 9:30 a.m.

Joe decided to walk over to the auto repair shop where the meetings were held. Maybe he could catch Phil before the service began.

The door to the building was locked when Joe arrived, and his knock was answered by the shop owner. The man told him that he could wait in the back yard for the Meades to come. Then the man went back into his living quarters next to the shop.

About five minutes later, Phil and Lisa arrived. The shop owner told them that someone had already arrived, so they went out back. They immediately recognized Joe and walked over to greet him.

"We're glad you decided to join us this morning!" said Phil.

Joe tried to smile in response, then looked at Phil and said, "I was wondering if I could talk with you for a few minutes before the service begins."

"Certainly," Phil replied. "Maybe we should step into the shop because people will be starting to come pretty quickly." He turned to his wife and said, "Lisa, do you mind?"

"No, that's fine. I'll just work on getting everything set up for the service."

Joe followed Phil around the side of the shop to the front door and entered it. Phil turned to Joe and waited for him to speak.

"I don't know exactly what to say, but I need to talk to someone, and I thought of you," Joe began hesitantly.

"I'm glad you did," said Phil, hoping that he could deal with whatever problem was on Joe's mind.

Joe continued, "The time that I came to your Bible study, you talked about Jonah, and how he was trying to run from doing the right thing. I guess I feel a little like Jonah."

Joe stopped talking, not sure how to express the thoughts and emotions that were churning inside him.

Phil studied him for a moment, then simply asked, "Why is that?"

"A few years ago I was involved in a crime. Not directly, but a man was shot. He—died."

Joe looked at Phil to see how he reacted to the statement. He couldn't quite interpret the expression, but it wasn't one of shock or loathing, so he decided to continue.

"I was driving around with a friend of mine, and we were both high. I dared him to rob a drugstore, and he said that it would be hard to do without a gun. I had my father's gun along. My father didn't know I had it. Anyway, this friend went in and I stayed in the van. A few minutes later, I heard a gunshot and he came running out. He told me that he had accidentally shot a man. Nothing happened for a few months. But when I heard that my friend was arrested by the police, I decided that it was time to leave home. He's in jail with a fifteen year sentence."

"And that's why you're in Mexico?" Phil asked.

"I spent a few years in San Diego without any problem, but someone I used to know has been trying to track me down, and I think it's because of my part in the crime. I don't know if the police are involved yet or not. I'm an accessory to the crime, but I don't want to go to prison. The hardest part is that I've got a wife, and she doesn't know anything about all this."

Surprise registered on Phil's face.

"I didn't realized you were married. Is your wife here in Mexico?" Phil asked.

"No, she's in San Diego, at least as far as I know. I haven't talked to her since I left several months ago, and she doesn't know where I am."

"Did you leave her any word, or does she think you might be dead?"

"I wrote her a note telling her I wished I could take her with me."

Phil gave Joe a sharp look and said, "Why couldn't you?"

"How could I take her with me when I'm living this kind of life? When I'm running from the law?"

Phil softened his tone and asked, "Do you love her?"

Joe's agony was so intense that he couldn't take offense at the question.

"I miss her a lot more than I thought I would. But, I love her enough to live without her, to spare her from a dead-end future."

Phil thought for a moment then asked, "Don't you think that your wife deserves to know the truth about you and your past? Then she can decide for herself what kind of future she wants. If she loves you at all she must be heartbroken not knowing where you are."

Joe stuffed his hands into his pockets and began to pace.

"If I go back I'll eventually end up in jail, which would be worse for Margaret than not knowing where I am."

"I'm not at all sure about that, Joe," Phil replied. "People usually choose an unpleasant truth over uncertainty. Why don't you at least let her know where you are?"

Joe continued pacing and didn't answer right away.

Phil looked at his watch and said, "I'm really sorry to say this, but the service will be starting soon and I need to get back in there. Can you come over to our apartment afterwards and we can talk some more?"

Joe stopped pacing and said, "Thank you for listening to me. I think I will stay for the service, but I don't think I'll come over afterwards. I've made up my mind about the situation."

Joe abruptly turned away and walked out the door, leaving Phil to follow behind with his would-be question unanswered.

TWENTY-SEVEN

CAROL AND PAUL WALKED UP THE DRIVEWAY of Margaret's house. Finding the door wide open to let in the summer breeze, Carol stuck her head inside.

"Greta, we're here!"

"Hi, guys! Come on in," Margaret called from her bedroom. "I'm just changing into something cooler. The heat has really been bothering me. I'll be right out."

"There's no hurry," Carol replied as she and Paul sat down on the couch. "Since it's a Sunday, most of the stores are just opening now anyway."

Margaret came out from the bedroom wearing shorts and a sleeveless maternity top. Her cheeks were pink and her forehead damp with perspiration.

"Have you two eaten lunch yet? I can make some sandwiches."

Paul replied, "We stopped for a hamburger after church."

"Well then, I guess we're ready to go," Margaret said, putting on her sandals.

"Need some help?" Carol asked with a smile, as she saw how difficult it was for Margaret to bend over.

"In another month or so, I won't even be able to find my feet much less get shoes on them!" Margaret replied as she finally got the buckles clasped.

"Do you mind if Paul stays here to study?" Carol asked. "He's got a test tomorrow, and I don't think he's that interested in shopping for a crib and baby outfits anyhow."

"That's fine," Margaret said with a grin. "I suppose he would get tired of hearing how 'adorable' everything is."

Carol said, "I was thinking that we could bring back some ingredients for pizza, and we could have homemade pizzas later on. Paul is quite a chef, and makes the best pizza around."

"So you're a good cook," Margaret teased them. "Now I know why Carol is so interested in you. Whenever she offered to make dinner, I remember eating a lot of macaroni and cheese."

"Macaroni and cheese may not be gourmet food, but it's better than a diet of french fries and chocolate chip cookies!" Carol retorted. "Some people are so ungrateful!"

"Well I think pizza sounds like a good idea," Paul interjected. "It's probably not as good as Carol makes it sound, but I think it beats macaroni or french fries."

Joe waited through the end of the worship service, then left before Phil had the opportunity to approach him. He felt as though a heavy weight had been lifted off of him. Normally he walked with his head down, to avoid meeting people's eyes. This time, however, he stood tall and smiled at the people who crossed his path.

He would call Margaret and tell her why he left, and the risk he faced of imprisonment. He would let her know how much he loved her, how strongly he missed her, and together they could make decisions about the future.

Finding a cafe with a sign saying, "Servicio de Larga Distancia," Joe went in to make the call. He didn't have long distance service with his apartment phone, never having needed it before. The only phone calls he received were occasional work questions or problems. After the second try, the operator was able to make the connection. The phone rang several times, and then was answered just as Joe had given up hope.

Startled, Joe heard a male voice answer, "Hello?"

"I'm sorry, the operator must have connected me to the wrong number," Joe said.

"This is Margaret Bechmann's number," replied Paul before Joe could hang up.

"Who are you?" Joe asked in puzzlement.

"My name is Paul, and I'm . . . uh . . . a friend of Margaret's."

"Well I want to talk to Margaret."

"She's not here right now. She's out shopping and will be back in a few hours. Can I take a message?"

A man in his house while Margaret was out shopping? He certainly was smooth, asking Joe to leave a message. Anger welled up inside of him.

"I'm Margaret's husband and I want to know what you're doing there."

"Margaret's husband—Oh! She's been trying to find out where you went. Where are you?"

"I'm not telling you where I am because it's none of your business. It didn't take Margaret long to move on to someone new. But she's still legally my wife."

"You've got it all wrong," Paul exclaimed, flustered. "Let me explain it to you. I met Margaret through Carol—I have been dating her, and Margaret and Carol wanted to go—"

Paul's voice trailed off as he heard the line go dead.

"Oh no!" Paul groaned out loud. "I think I really blew it!"

TWENTY-EIGHT

"HEY BUDDY, HOW'S IT GOING?"

Rod was sitting in the prison visitor's room when Carl came in, escorted by a guard.

"I'm glad to see you Rod, it's been a while."

Carl sat down across from Rod.

"Yeah, I've been kind of busy lately. I bought a new car that I've been fixing up. I'll bring a picture next time. I gotta have something classy to take Stephanie out with. I've been seeing her for the last few months. She's real good looking. I'll bring you a picture of her too."

Normally Carl had no interest in Rod's cars or women, but his attitude toward Rod had been changing and he wanted to deepen the friendship.

"What kind of person is Stephanie?"

"She's got long blonde hair and blue eyes and she was a runner-up at some beauty pageant. She probably would have won if it wasn't for the talent portion."

"What's her personality like?"

"She laughs a lot. Sometimes she's kinda touchy, but I just tell her I love her and she's O.K."

"Do you mean it when you say it?"

Rod was taken aback. It was unusual enough for Carl to ask questions about his girlfriends, but an interest in honesty was definitely out of character.

"Oh, I probably do mean it at the time, but I'm not ready to get too serious yet," Rod said with a laugh. He changed subjects. "It's too bad that José left before you could get the police interested in the situation. Do you want me to check back at the hotel where he worked and see if they've heard from him?"

"No, Rod. I'm not going to try to do that anymore. I've decided to forgive José."

Rod's face expressed the astonishment he felt.

"Forgive him? What's wrong with you! All you've talked about over the last six years is getting your revenge!"

Rod spoke loudly, causing others in the room to look his direction.

Carl looked at Rod a moment before speaking, trying to weigh his words.

"I want you to know something that has happened to me since you last visited. I became a Christian."

Rod was incredulous.

"A Christian? *You* got *religion*?"

Carl looked embarrassed. "I wouldn't have believed it myself a few months ago. But I prayed with Robin, a guy who has been visiting me as part of a class project. All I can say is that I know God is real. When I talk to Him I can feel his presence."

"You're talking to God? Next thing I know you're going to think you *are* God. Listen, man, you've gotta be careful. Prison can do some strange things to people."

"Don't worry, Rod," Carl said with a laugh. "I haven't gone over the edge. I feel better than I ever did before. I'm learning a lot about how to deal with problems by reading my Bible and talking to Robin. Knowing Jesus gives you a different perspective in life. The Bible says that you need to think about others, not just yourself. I'm learning to love people."

Carl stopped talking, seeing that Rod was shaking his head.

"I just don't get it," Rod said. "You're not the same person at all. How can you be so different in just a few months?"

Carl smiled and said, "That's what I'm trying to tell you. Jesus has changed me. But we can talk more about this later. Tell me about your new car."

Rod was a lot more comfortable discussing cars than religion, and his enthusiasm over his recent acquisition was obvious. After a lengthy discussion of his car and his job, Rod decided to leave before the subject of Carl's change was brought up again.

Carl said, "Thanks for the visit, Rod. Don't let that new girlfriend of yours keep you away so long next time."

"Yeah—I'll catch you later," Rod replied.

He left the room escorted by a guard, and as he walked down the hall he shook his head and muttered, "I don't believe it."

TWENTY-NINE

MARGARET HAD NEVER BEEN TO MEXICO BEFORE. She had never joined Carol's shopping expeditions to Tijuana. When she had time, she was broke, and when she had money, it was from working extra shifts. Plus there were visits to her family and dates with Joe to keep her busy. When she suggested to Joe that they try a restaurant she heard had great lobster, he said he didn't like seafood. And Joe hadn't been interested in visiting his Mexican relatives.

Margaret wasn't sure what to expect in crossing the border, because Carol always walked across and used public transportation to get around. So, she came prepared for any difficulties that might occur. She had located her birth certificate, obtained a passport and purchased Mexican auto insurance. Isabela warned her that the Mexican government did not recognize foreign car insurance, and that without proper coverage, visitors could end up in jail after an accident.

The documents were beside her in the passenger's seat. Along with them was a jug of bottled water and a glass, a map of the Baja Peninsula and a Spanish phrase book.

San Ysidro, the border town on the California side was behind her, and Tijuana ahead. Margaret was so busy dodging cars and reading signs that she almost exited into the "park and walk" area by mistake.

It was almost a disappointment to her that crossing the border was so easy. Margaret was simply waved through—no questions, no checking the car. Looking at the lanes of traffic at a standstill from the other direction, however, caused Margaret to realize that the return trip wouldn't be so easy.

If there was a way to avoid downtown Tijuana, Margaret missed it, and she ended up in the middle of the biggest traffic jam in the smallest area she had ever seen. Trying to block out the cacophony of noise, she concentrated on navigating in the heavy traffic.

Rundown storefronts with enormous, gaudy signs were crowded so closely together that Margaret began to feel claustrophobic. Most of the businesses appeared to be trying to attract U.S. dollars. "Gifts," "Body Work," and "Divorce" were among the enticements written in English. To her relief, Margaret finally saw a sign for the road to Tecate which she knew was the direction of Mexicali.

The traffic thinned as soon as Margaret got outside of Tijuana. She decided then and there to take a different way back home.

"Home," she mused.

Even though she was only a few miles away from San Diego, she felt as though it could have been a thousand. Her Spanish vocabulary was almost non-existent, and she had been warned against driving alone in Mexico.

When Isabela learned that Margaret decided to travel to Mexico in hopes of finding Joe, she was quick to make arrangements for Margaret to stay with her sister, Juanita Rodriguez.

"It's not a good idea for a young woman to travel alone, especially in your condition," Isabela had said. "My sister and her family welcome you to stay as long as you feel you need to."

Margaret's parents had been upset. They thought it unwise for Margaret to travel to Mexico while pregnant, especially since she was so unlikely to find Joe. But they were won over by Margaret's calm manner when she explained that it was the only "lead" she had to finding Joe, and that she could never be happy if she didn't at least try to find him. The fact that Juanita's husband was a doctor also helped to ease their fears. Margaret was grateful that her parents chose to be supportive of her decision, and grateful also for a gift of money from them for travel expenses.

Margaret's employer was willing to grant her a leave of absence after hearing of her predicament. She was able to begin her six months maternity leave early. Although that would leave only four months after the baby was due to be born, Margaret couldn't wait any later than that to travel to Mexico in case the baby arrived early. She wanted to have a full month to look for Joe.

"How do you think you could possibly find Joe, assuming he is in Mexico?" Carol asked when Margaret had stopped by for a visit.

"Joe knows the hotel business, and he's most familiar with the Baja, so that's where I'm going to concentrate my search."

Carol's concern was evident.

"Why don't you get the names and phone numbers of hotels and resorts in Baja California and call, rather than traveling when you're pregnant? You can get really sick from the food and water down there if you're not careful. You have to think of the baby."

"First of all, I've heard that it's often difficult to get through to Mexico by phone. Second, I don't know if Joe is using his real name. Whether or not he is, if the word reaches him that someone is asking for him by name he might leave. He thinks the worst of me now, and may not want to hear from me. If I go down there, I can show a photo to the employees of various hotels. Also, I'm going to be staying in Joe's Aunt's home. I shouldn't have a problem with the food or water there, and anyway, I'll be careful. I know this sounds like a long-shot, but I have to try if I'm ever going to have any peace of mind."

"What if Joe comes back or tries to call again while you're in Mexico?"

This was Carol's last attempt to persuade Margaret not to go.

"I'll have to take that chance," said Margaret with a shrug of her shoulders. "I'm going to leave a note for him in case he would come back home, and I bought an answering machine to take messages."

In the end, Carol gave her a hug and said to be careful and that she would pray for Margaret.

The hour-long drive to Tecate on Highway 2 calmed her nerves a little. Despite the large amount of litter strewn about, the rolling hills were pretty and Margaret enjoyed seeing the grazing cattle and olive orchards.

The hills gave way to mountains as the elevation increased. Margaret was now on the western slopes of the Peninsular Range Mountains. Enormous boulders were everywhere, causing Margaret to wonder if they ever came loose and rolled into the traffic. The boulders near the road were covered with messages and graffiti, some of which was translatable into any language.

Margaret was almost to Tecate when she saw a Pemex station. She needed some gas and to use the bathroom.

"Lleno, por favor," she said to the attendant, hoping that he would understand her request to fill up the tank. She wasn't sure she was pronouncing the phrase from her travelers' handbook correctly.

Margaret handed the attendant a $20 bill, having heard that U.S. dollars were always welcome. She received change in pesos. Margaret wasn't sure what the exchange rate was and didn't even know how much gas had been put in. She just hoped that the attendant was honest.

"¿Donde está el baño?"

Again, Margaret relied on the handbook. The attendant replied something in Spanish and pointed to the side of the gas station.

Margaret pulled her car over and entered what she hoped to be the woman's restroom. It was dirty and there wasn't a mirror. Worse, she discovered too late that there wasn't any toilet paper.

When she reached the center of town, Margaret stopped to find something to eat. The streets formed a square, which contained a park on the inside and various businesses on the outside.

Margaret saw what looked like a snack bar and walked over to it. She saw a wide variety of ice cream bars and frozen fruit bars, as well as milk shakes and fruit juice drinks. She tried asking in English what the flavors were, but resorted to guessing and pointing when her efforts at verbal communication proved unsuccessful. Margaret brought the shake she purchased back to the car. A taste proved it to be strawberry as she hoped for, and the added cinnamon made it especially delicious.

Margaret continued east toward Mexicali. The map showed it being only ninety miles from Tecate, but she knew that the mountains would slow things down a little. She wasn't prepared for how difficult the drive was, however.

The view was as spectacular as it was alarming. Margaret wasn't sure what "Despacio" meant, but she drove especially cautiously whenever she saw it on a sign. From the number of cars littering the mountainside, and the white crosses marking their descent, it appeared that many a driver had not taken the dangerous curves seriously.

As she descended toward Mexicali, Margaret was aware of the desertous climate. The air was getting so stifling hot that she had to roll up the windows and turn on the air conditioning. Even then, she could feel the heat of the sun through the windows. The mountains no longer had any vegetation. She passed a sign for

Laguna Salada, but all that Margaret could see was a dry, empty area where she guessed a lake might have been.

Exhausted and hungry from the long, treacherous drive, Margaret was glad to finally arrive in Mexicali. She had been so sure of herself when convincing her parents and Carol that this was the right thing to do. Now that she was actually doing it, however, she had to admit that she was scared. What if she did get sick? What if she did have problems with her pregnancy? What if she couldn't find Joe? What if she did and he didn't love her any more? The "what-ifs" flooded her mind and filled her with anxiety.

Margaret got out the directions and located the Rodriguez home without major difficulty. She was glad that Isabela had written out landmarks to go by, as many streets lacked signs, and there was a spot where several streets came together, circling around a statue. Margaret wondered if the statue depicted a hero of the Mexican Revolution, and wished she had paid more attention in her social studies classes.

The house was attractively designed, located in an upper class residential neighborhood. When she knocked on the door, it was answered by a woman who bore a striking resemblance to Isabela, although a few years younger.

"Come in—come in, please!"

Juanita spoke English, but not fluently.

"You are Margaret?"

"Yes, I am," she replied. "And you must be Juanita. Thank you so much for letting me stay with you!"

Juanita spoke in Spanish to the three children behind her who appeared to range in ages from about eight to fourteen. Apparently they were being told who Margaret was and given some instructions concerning her.

Juanita turned back to Margaret with a smile and asked, "You have bags? Herman takes them to bedroom. Please sit. I get you lemonade."

Juanita motioned Margaret into a chair. Margaret leaned back and shut her eyes for a moment. She felt relieved that she had made the trip without difficulty, but apprehensive about the task before her.

Juanita returned with the glass of lemonade which Margaret gratefully accepted. Although her thoughts were drawn to the uncertainty of the future, Margaret determined not to look too far ahead. She would concentrate on one step at a time.

THIRTY

MARGARET WAS RELIEVED TO FIND MEXICALI SO DIFFERENT from Tijuana. It wasn't such a tourist town, and other than the rows of shacks and shanties that lined the outskirts of the city, it wasn't too different from home. Without any ocean breeze to cool it off, however, the summer heat was almost unbearable.

Margaret spent the first week in Mexicali visiting the larger hotels in the area, although Juanita thought it unlikely that Joe would be so close to relatives if he didn't want to be seen. Margaret dreaded traveling back through the mountains, however, and she felt it would be the best place to start as long as she was staying there. But nobody she spoke with recognized Joe from the photograph, or had heard his name.

It was a tedious task, as many people did not speak English. She guessed that several hotel employees wanted to know why she was asking about someone, but she couldn't understand them, and they didn't seem interested in waiting while she looked up words in her dictionary.

Tijuana also proved to be a disappointment. Juanita offered to spend the week-end in Tijuana with Margaret, having some business there and not wanting her to travel alone. Gratefully, Margaret accepted the offer, despite the short length of time she would have to look. With Tijuana being the biggest tourist town in the Baja there were an enormous number of hotels and motels of every kind and variety. Margaret felt let down after she had visited many of the hotels without finding Joe. Tijuana was so close to San Diego, however, that Margaret could come back after the baby was born to look some more.

The next city Margaret would visit was Ensenada, which had been growing recently as a tourist town. San Felipe was the last place she would try. Juanita cautioned her against traveling south to the tip of the peninsula, due to the distance and the desertous conditions.

"Is no good, Margaret. Is hard to get gas—sometimes people get lost and die. Is long trip there, maybe two or three nights."

Margaret reluctantly had to agree. There were more hotels and motels than she could visit anyway. After San Felipe, she would be out of time and would need to head back to San Diego to wait for the baby to be born.

The possibility of leaving for home without finding Joe was something that Margaret couldn't think about. She just had to find him!

This time Juanita was not able to accompany Margaret. Her youngest was sick and needed her mother's care. Margaret didn't want to waste any time, so decided to go alone to Ensenada despite the long, difficult drive through the mountains again. Hearing how crowded hotels could get in Ensenada, she had reservations made in advance and didn't want to cancel them.

Just outside of Ensenada, Margaret was greeted by an unusual sight. A horse must have been struck by a vehicle, and was lying dead in the middle of the street. No damaged truck or car was in sight, and Margaret hoped that the driver had made out better than the horse. Then and there, Margaret decided to heed Juanita's warning not to drive at night because of animals wandering across the highways.

When Margaret finally arrived in Ensenada, she checked into the "El Camino Real" hotel where she would stay for at least two nights. She went into her room to freshen up a little before starting the task. She felt relieved to be near the ocean once again, as the pleasant breeze and comfortable temperature buoyed her spirits.

Margaret went back to the front desk of El Camino Real and asked to see the manager. A short, balding man who appeared to be in his forties came out of an office to see her.

"What can I do for you, Señora?" he asked politely in English, much to Margaret's relief. She had heard that English was frequently spoken in Ensenada because of the large number of U.S. tourists.

"I am wondering if you have an employee here by the name of Joe or José Bechmann?"

The manager looked puzzled. "We do not have any person working here with that name. Why is it that you want to find this person?"

When asked that question, Margaret gave her stock answer of "for personal reasons," leaving the questioner to speculate all he wanted.

She showed him a photograph of Joe and asked, "Have you seen this man anywhere?"

The manager took the photograph and studied it for a moment.

"The man in the picture looks familiar, although I can't remember where I would have seen him." He took a second long look then handed the photograph back to Margaret saying, "Come back later and I might remember where I saw this man."

Excited that she was on the right track, Margaret thanked the manager and left to visit other hotels. Her thoughts tumbled around rapidly. So Joe had been in Ensenada, but when? Was he still here? At least there was some confirmation that she was looking in the right area.

It was early evening by the time she had spoken with employees at five more hotels. The only encouragement was that another manager also thought that Joe's face looked familiar, but couldn't say anything beyond that. Exhausted from the long day, Margaret decided to return to the hotel where she was staying. She would eat supper at the adjoining restaurant before going to bed.

Fortunately, the restaurant listed the meals in English as well as Spanish, enabling Margaret to order a chicken dinner. A lot of Mexican food didn't sit well this late in her pregnancy. While Margaret ate, a mariachi band strolled through the restaurant, singing and playing instruments. She noticed a couple next to her enjoying the lively entertainment, and felt a sharp pang of sadness. She ate a lonely meal, then went to her room.

Margaret turned the television set on for companionship. Although U.S. programs were available, she tuned into what looked like a variety show in Spanish. It was entertaining to watch, even without understanding everything going on. The television host's animated performance was exceeded only by the audience's enthusiastic participation.

Before long, however, Margaret turned off the television to go to sleep. She wanted to get an early start. Although it was hard for her to fall asleep all alone in a foreign country, she calmed her anxiety with the thought that maybe tomorrow she would find Joe. Beyond that event she refused to dwell, and eventually her thoughts quieted enough to fall soundly asleep.

La Paloma was Margaret's third stop the next morning. Outside the hotel was a wedding party sitting in horse-drawn carriages. Peach-colored dresses fluttered in the breeze, catching Margaret's eye. She looked at the bride's face, brimming with excitement, and wondered what marriage would hold in store for her. Margaret went to the front desk and asked to see the manager.

"I am Señor Martínez. I am an owner of the hotel. How may I help you?"

Margaret took out the picture of Joe and handed it to him.

"Can you tell me if you recognize this man?" she asked hopefully.

She wanted to try the photograph before trying the name.

"Sure, I know this man," Señor Martínez replied immediately. "He is Joe Bechmann."

Excitement flooded through Margaret and she excitedly asked, "Does he work here? Where can I find him?"

Margaret's enthusiasm sparked curiosity in Señor Martínez. But noting her condition, he felt it better not to ask why she was looking for him.

"I do not know where you can find him. He was a manager here, and a good one, but he quit working just yesterday. He said he had to leave, but didn't tell me where or why, and I make it a practice not to ask too many questions. I will miss having him here."

With desperation in her voice, Margaret asked, "Do you know where he has been living? Do you have any idea how I might reach him?"

Señor Martínez normally did not give out any personal information on his employees, but he noted the look of pleading in Margaret's eyes, and with a deep sigh relented.

"I have his phone number and address here, and you may use the phone here if you would like."

Señor Martínez wrote down the number and address for her and brought her into his office to use the phone. Margaret dialed the number and let it ring for a couple of minutes. She finally put the receiver down and walked out of the office where Señor Martínez was waiting in order to give her privacy.

"There was no answer. Thank you for letting me try." Margaret tried to smile at his kindness, but tears were in her eyes. She continued, "I will drive to this address and see if he has moved out."

"Would you like me to give him a message if he calls or stops by for some reason?" Señor Martínez asked with compassion in his voice.

Margaret thought for a moment and replied, "You could tell him that Margaret is looking for him. That she—that I—need to find him. I'm staying in Mexicali for another week at his aunt and uncle's home and then returning home. Do you want me to write that down?"

"No, Señora Margaret, I will remember that message. I wish you good fortune in finding Joe."

Margaret thanked him, then left. She hoped she would be able to follow the directions the owner of the hotel gave her. If there were signs that Joe had not moved out yet, she would stay and wait until he came back. If he was gone already, maybe his neighbors or landlord would know where he went to. She just had to find him!

When Margaret found the apartment, the door was locked. A young girl stuck her head out of the door down the hall, curious about who was knocking so persistently.

"Do you know where the man who lives here is?" Margaret asked in English doubting that the girl understood what she was asking.

The girl went back into her apartment and shut the door. Margaret sighed and decided to see if the girl's parents were home to ask. Just as she reached up to knock on the door, it opened.

A middle-aged looking woman asked her in English who she wanted to see.

"Joe Bechmann. I knocked on the door of his apartment, but there was no answer. Do you know where he is?"

The woman looked her up and down before answering.

"Joe Bechmann does not rent here anymore. He left this morning. He did not tell us where he was going."

In desperation, Margaret asked, "Don't you have any idea where he might have gone? It's very important. If you can help me, I'll pay you!"

The woman frowned in disapproval and said, "He did not say and I did not ask."

Margaret's disappointment was overwhelming. She didn't say anything further to the woman, but turned away with tears blinding her eyes. She walked down the hall and out the front entrance. She would have gotten into her car if she knew where to go. Instead she sat on the steps outside the apartment.

"Oh, God," she whispered, "you have to help me find him. I'm too close now to give up, but I don't know where to look. Please help me, God."

Margaret decided to wait for a while outside the apartment. Maybe she would meet a neighbor who knew something. Somehow, she would find Joe. She had to.

THIRTY-ONE

THE MORNING MAIL HAD BROUGHT JOE'S LAST PAYCHECK, which he had been waiting for. His few belongings were already packed into a duffel bag. What he couldn't fit, he wouldn't bring back with him. Although he had purchased some clothing and a few household items out of necessity, Joe had not bought much in Mexico. There really was no point. Likewise, his apartment had not undergone any heavy use, and it was simply a matter of a little sweeping and he had been ready to go.

Joe walked to the bank, where he cashed his last paycheck and withdrew his savings in U.S. dollars. Although Joe's income was small by American standards, he had been able to save some money out of each paycheck because his living expenses were minimal. This money had been added to the savings Joe brought with him to Mexico.

It devastated Joe to think he had spent the last few years of his life working so hard to save money for the future, and now he wouldn't be needing it. He didn't have a future anymore. Without Margaret's love, he had no hope. He still couldn't believe she was seeing another man. Although she didn't deserve it, he would send the money to her. He had nothing else to use it for.

Joe put the money into his pocket, and decided to stop for lunch at one of his favorite cafes before catching the bus out of Ensenada.

As Joe walked to the cafe he thought about what he would do next. He considered confronting Margaret before turning himself in to the police. He wanted to demand an explanation from her for her unfaithfulness. After thinking about how painful it would be, however, he decided against it. Writing a letter would be easier. He would explain why he had to leave, emphasizing that when he tried to tell her earlier, she walked out on him.

The cafe was crowded that day, so the service took longer than usual. It didn't bother Joe, however, as he allowed extra time to get to the bus. He tried drafting a letter to Margaret, but the right words just wouldn't come to mind. When the food arrived, he put down his pen and the napkin he was scribbling on, and tried to enjoy it, but it seemed as though he was eating his "last meal" before the firing squad.

After finishing a burrito and beans, Joe paid for his meal and started for the bus stop. Suddenly he stopped in mid-stride, almost causing a couple behind him to walk into him. He left his passport under his mattress! How ironic that after running from U.S. authorities to Mexico, without his passport, he might not be able to get back into the country. Joe got turned around and headed back toward his apartment. He was actually glad of a brief reprieve from the task ahead.

A few minutes later Joe turned the corner on the block of the apartment building. He saw a woman sitting on the steps, hunched over with her arms around her knees. She was wearing a denim jumper. As realization dawned on him, he slowed his pace and then stopped walking altogether. It was Margaret.

Joe was shocked. He didn't know what to do. A desire to talk with Margaret battled with his resolve to put her out of his mind and heart. He took a step forward to go over and speak his mind to her, then changed his mind and took a step back to move out of her view behind a battered pick-up truck that was parked in the street. Then he stepped out half-way to get a partial view of Margaret.

As if sensing she was being watched, Margaret lifted up her head and looked around. Joe ducked back behind the pick-up. A minute later, however, his curiosity got the best of him, and he took another look. Margaret was standing, discreetly stretching her muscles as though she had been sitting for too long. Joe's jaw dropped in disbelief. She had gotten herself pregnant.

From her appearance, Margaret hadn't wasted any time in finding comfort in another man's arms when Joe left. Joe was enraged. He must have been fooling himself all along in thinking that she loved him. He had actually believed that his marriage was going to solve his problems. Completely disillusioned, Joe turned and walked back the way he had come. He would cross the border as thousands of other people did each year—illegally.

THIRTY-TWO

ROSE PUT THE PHONE DOWN. The prison chaplain had called on Carl Milford's behalf to request a meeting with her. She formed his name with her lips and involuntarily shuddered. Even after all this time, saying his name was still a struggle.

Almost seven years had passed since her husband was killed. Seven years of emptiness—seven years of raising three boys without a father. Daniel was sixteen now. He reminded her of Simon more each day.

She did her best, but Rose knew that the boys needed a lot of parental guidance to survive their teen years. She didn't know how she could give any more. After working hard each day to make ends meet, she didn't have much time or energy left for parenting.

Anger had helped her to make it so far. It gave her the grit and determination needed to survive when she wanted to die. But she hadn't fully understood the cost. It was a trade of emotions. In exchange for anger, Rose gave up sorrow. She refused comfort when it had been given, and did not allow herself to be weak. But like clay when baked, with the hardness came brittleness.

Love had also been bartered. Rose didn't feel the acute pain of loss, but her constant companion was a deadness in her soul. Joy was non-existent. Although she did her best for her sons, she was no longer able to take delight in them. She had struggled, and she had survived, but her life had no vitality.

Even the pleasure of visualizing Carl being repaid for his murderous act was gone. She still hated him, but the fire had burnt low, leaving only a few glowing embers in the midst of ashes.

"Being sorry can't ever replace my husband," she told the chaplain.

He said he understood, but encouraged her to consider it.

"Sometimes hearing a person's regret helps to heal the hurt they have caused."

In the end she agreed to a visit. She wasn't sure why, but if for no other reason, she might be able to focus her hate toward him better after meeting him.

Rose had never been inside a prison before. It was an eerie sensation to be closed in behind two sets of security doors. She felt a sense of panic rise when she was searched for weapons or contraband.

All three boys wanted to come with, but Rose had been firm in her denial.

"This is something that I have to do myself," she told them. "You're not old enough."

"But Mom, I'm sixteen," Daniel protested. "I'm practically an adult!"

Rose's resolve faded as she saw the chaplain approach. Having at least Daniel along might have given her more courage.

"I'm Arnie Youngquist, the chaplain," he said as he shook her hand.

Noticing how clammy her hand was, Arnie said, "We'll keep it brief. If you feel uncomfortable, we can leave. Just let me know."

As they headed for Arnie's office, Rose braced herself for seeing Carl. She took one of two seats in front of the chaplain's desk, and in doing so positioned the chairs further apart. They didn't wait long before Carl arrived. He walked in, nervously nodding a greeting to the chaplain.

Carl looked at Rose and said, "Thank you for coming."

Rose didn't respond and simply stared at him. She was almost disappointed that he was nice-looking, not like the drugged-out murderous youth she had remembered. Carl looked again at the chaplain, who motioned him to sit down in the empty chair.

"I asked you to come," he began haltingly, "because I wanted to tell you—I want you to know how sorry I am about your husband."

Rose continued staring at him, giving him no acknowledgement that she had heard him.

"Mrs. Felder, would you like to leave now?" the chaplain asked, breaking the silence.

She slowly turned her gaze to him and answered, "No, I want to hear what else he has to say."

Her eyes riveted back onto Carl's face.

"I don't know if it helps you any," Carl continued, "but the shooting was an accident. I didn't intend to kill anyone."

Carl saw Rose visibly tighten.

"I'm not trying to say that I don't deserve to be where I am. I fully intended to rob the drugstore and I had a gun. I was high on drugs. I tripped and your husband tried to grab the gun. I got it first and . . ."

His voice trailed off. Rose spoke then, her voice sounding as though each word were an effort.

"Why apologize now, after seven years?"

"I didn't think I had anything to apologize for before," Carl explained, hunting for the right words to say. "I was a different person. I was angry for being in prison and I blamed everyone else. It's in the last few months that I've changed. I realize now that I was the one responsible for ending up here. I am able to understand some of the pain that I've caused you and your family. I believe that God has forgiven me for what I did. It's the first time I've felt at peace with myself since—"

"I've heard enough," Rose interrupted. "I'm ready to go now."

She took some satisfaction in watching Carl cringe at her next words. "You have no right in talking about forgiveness after what you did!"

"Mrs. Felder," Arnie interjected. "we agreed to be courteous."

Rose stood up and opened the door. "I'm finished," she said.

Rose looked back at Carl who didn't respond. He kept his gaze lowered and his face a mask. Arnie stood up and came around his desk.

He placed a hand on Carl's shoulder and said, "Why don't you wait here? I'll be back in a few minutes."

The chaplain then followed Rose out the door. She was standing in the hall, turned away from the office, with her arms crossed in front of her.

"Would you like to talk?" Arnie asked as they walked to the front door.

"How can he say that it took him all these years to realize that murder is wrong?" Rose demanded.

"I don't want to make light of his crime, but I do believe he has taken a big step. Many inmates never accept responsibility for what they have done."

"And how can he talk about forgiveness to me? To *me!?*"

"Mrs. Felder, I don't think that Carl was trying to anger you. He was trying to explain his motivation in requesting this meeting. I'm sorry that you didn't find it to be helpful."

Rose would have continued, but she was too exhausted. Instead, she walked the rest of the way in silence. Was it possible that God had forgiven him? Would a God of justice overlook murder?

Rose didn't know. The God she believed in was a judge. Good things were given to the righteous, and mercy to those who deserved it. Bad people were punished for their deeds. But that God was distant from Rose, and she wasn't sure anymore that he even existed. After all, He was the one who let Simon be taken away from her.

Rose turned to the chaplain as they approached the exit.

"I don't know if this meeting was helpful to either one of us, but I'm not sorry I came. He wasn't what I expected. . . ."

Rose shook the chaplain's hand, then was escorted out of the prison by a guard. As she walked to her car, she tried to rekindle her anger toward Carl, but she just didn't have the energy anymore. With her defenses down, a thought wormed its way into her consciousness. She attempted to push it away, but it persisted.

Was the anger worth the sacrifice?

The next day, Rose called her mother-in-law and asked her to come along to the cemetery where Simon was buried. The request surprised Helen, because Rose had not visited the cemetery since the day of the funeral. On the way, Rose stopped at a florist's shop and purchased an arrangement of seven roses. "One for each year Simon has been gone," Rose explained to Helen.

When they arrived, Rose walked immediately to the grave site, leaving Helen to follow behind as her arthritic knees allowed. She placed the flowers in front of the headstone, then knelt down, unmindful of her clothes getting dirty. The tears began to trickle, gradually turning into a flood. Helen approached Rose, and carefully knelt down next to her.

"I loved him so much!" said Rose, as if acknowledging the fact for the first time.

"I know you did," responded Helen. "You were a good wife to him, and I know he loved you dearly."

"Why did he have to die?"

Helen couldn't answer the question, so she put her arm around Rose instead.

"It's been so hard!" Rose exclaimed as a fresh wave of tears broke forth.

"I know it has," her mother-in-law said simply as Rose turned to her, crying on her shoulder.

For the first time, Rose experienced a small measure of comfort, and with it a small flicker of hope.

THIRTY-THREE

JOE HAD ONLY WALKED A COUPLE OF BLOCKS when he heard someone call his name. He looked up to see Phil Meade walking toward him. Of all the people he wasn't prepared to see on this day, Margaret was one and Phil was the other.

"I see you're still in Ensenada," Phil said as he got closer to Joe. "I hadn't seen you for a while, so I was wondering if you left town."

"I haven't yet, but I was just on my way," Joe said, turning slightly to show his duffel bag.

"You're returning to the U.S., then?"

"Yes. I decided that I'm going to talk to the police and tell them about my involvement with the crime."

Then the question that Joe was dreading came.

"What did you decide about your wife?"

Phil knew he was in very personal territory, but wanted to at least give Joe the opportunity to talk if he wanted to.

Joe debated what to say, then finally said, "She's here, but I can't talk to her. She doesn't know I saw her."

Phil didn't respond verbally, but at his look of surprise, Joe felt a need to continue.

"After I spoke with you last time, I called home. A guy answered and told me that Margaret was out shopping. I asked him who he was and he told me that he had been dating Margaret. That's when I hung up," Joe finished bitterly.

"So you think she's been unfaithful to you."

"I know it. When I saw her just now, she was obviously pregnant. I still can't believe she would do this to me."

"It must be a shock," Phil said shaking his head.

"What would you do?" Joe asked, seeing Phil's reaction.

Phil thought for a moment, then responded. "I guess I would be awfully curious about her reason for coming to Ensenada. Maybe she is sorry and wants to make amends."

"The only thing I've thought of is that she wants a divorce," Joe said. "But maybe you're right—maybe the guy left her and she wants me back."

"It would be worth talking to her to see what she has to say," Phil replied. "You're never going to discover what the situation really is unless you do."

Joe agonized over his choice, then finally said, "I think you're right. I do want to know what she has to say about all this. If Margaret's still there, I'll talk to her."

"Something else you may want to consider," Phil added, "is that infidelity doesn't necessarily have to end a marriage. Some couples survive the problem."

"It's hard to believe—but anyway, thanks for the advice."

Joe turned and walked quickly back toward his former residence.

Margaret was still sitting on the steps. As Joe approached her, she looked up.

"Joe! Oh, Joe!" Margaret screamed when she saw him. She ran over to him and threw her arms around him. "I found you—thank God I found you!"

Joe stood stiffly and didn't return the hug. "What are you doing here, Margaret?" he asked coolly.

"I found your parents, and your mother gave me the idea of looking for you in Mexico! I've been staying at your Aunt Juanita's house in Mexicali. I've been going to all the hotels in

Mexicali and Tijuana and Ensenada trying to track you down. I went to La Paloma and got your address, but when I got here you were already gone. I didn't know what to do! I just about gave up hope. But you're here, you're really here!"

Margaret began to sob as she held Joe even more tightly.

"Did Paul tell you that I called?" Joe practically spat out his name.

Margaret let go of Joe, took a step backwards and looked up at him. "Yes, Joe, he did—but it's not what you think. He told me that you misunderstood him, and thought he said he was dating me. He's going out with Carol! He came over with Carol, and decided to stay at the house while Carol and I went out shopping."

"But you're pregnant!"

"You think—Joe how could you think that! It's *your* baby!"

"My baby?" Joe was incredulous.

"Yes, yours. I was pregnant when you left but didn't know it yet."

Joe didn't respond right away and just looked at Margaret trying to take it all in.

"It was a surprise to me, too," Margaret said quietly. "I almost couldn't handle it."

"How do I know you're telling the truth?" Joe blurted out.

"You don't believe me? How can you say that!" Margaret burst into tears again. "How can you even think that of me!"

Joe saw hurt so deep in Margaret's face that he knew it couldn't be manufactured. He pulled Margaret into his arms.

"I should have trusted you. I'm sorry. I'm really sorry."

"I'm the one who needs to apologize for not trusting," Margaret replied. "I should have given you some time to tell me about the money. I shouldn't have left when we argued. I went to my parent's house. I was going to call you that night, but I ended up deciding not to. I'm so sorry!"

"Margaret, I have a lot of explaining to do," Joe responded. "I have to tell you why I left and what I'm doing in Mexico."

Margaret interrupted him. "Your mom told me that she thought you were connected with a crime. I don't care. It's over and done with. Just come back home."

"It's not that simple, Margaret. I've decided that I can't live this way, with the fear of being caught hanging over me. I've got to go back and own up to my involvement with the crime. You have to understand that we didn't intend to hurt anyone. It was just supposed to be a simple robbery. But a man was killed and I'm an accessory to the crime. I'm going to jail."

Margaret took hold of his hand and pleaded, "Oh Joe, please just come back. You don't have to turn yourself in. You might never get caught. We can worry about that later. I need you, Joe. Your baby needs you."

Margaret clung to him and sobbed almost hysterically, unmindful of the curious looks of the caretaker's wife and a few people passing by. Joe was more torn than he ever thought it possible to be. He held Margaret tightly against his chest, and for the first time in many years, tears ran down his cheeks.

In a voice hoarse with emotion he said, "Margaret, I really misjudged you. I hope you can forgive me. I want you to know that when I called that day, I was calling to tell you how much I loved you. I was planning on talking things over with you, to make plans for the future. . . ."

Margaret's words were muffled by Joe's shoulder. "Your future is with me, in our house in San Diego."

Trying to control his voice, Joe responded, "I can't promise to always be with you, but I'm here for you now. I'll do the best I can for you . . . and for the baby."

THIRTY-FOUR

UNCOMFORTABLE, MARGARET STIRRED IN HER SLEEP, waking up enough to feel relief in knowing that Joe was next to her. It was so good to have him home again. Every moment was savored during the three weeks since they returned to San Diego together.

Margaret willed her mind to return to slumber, when she suddenly realized what woke her in the first place.

"A contraction! The baby is ready to come!"

Margaret looked at the alarm clock next to her bed and timed the contraction. It wasn't very painful and it wasn't very long, but it was distinct. Margaret got out of bed to get a piece of paper and pen to keep track of the contractions. Her doctor had told her to come into the hospital when the contractions reached five minutes apart.

As she stood in the kitchen, Joe came out looking very unkempt with his hair standing up and his eyes half shut.

"What are you doing?" he mumbled.

Suppressing a laugh at how he looked, she walked over to him and gave him a big hug.

"I think it's time, Joe. I had a contraction and I want to keep track to see how far apart they are."

Joe sat down on a kitchen chair. He still wasn't used to the idea of Margaret being pregnant, much less becoming a father himself.

"You're sure?" he asked weakly.

"I'm not positive," answered Margaret. "You know I've never gone through this before. But it sure seems like the real thing!"

"Do you have everything packed for the hospital?"

"I left some things packed from going to Mexico. I forgot about packing a baby outfit, though. I'll have to get out one of the ones I bought. I didn't want to take a chance at guessing the sex wrong, so I didn't buy any pink or blue."

Margaret went into the second bedroom which was decorated to be a nursery. She was proud of herself for sewing curtains and bedding for the crib. The fabric had zoo animals in primary colors on it, and a matching border went around the top of the room.

The dresser was one that her parents were discarding. Carol helped Margaret repaint it and stencil animals on it. In the top drawer were five baby outfits and some diapers. Margaret selected a yellow one with a giraffe on the front, along with a pair of booties and a baby blanket she purchased at a garage sale. She brought them out to show Joe.

"Just think, in a few hours, we'll have a baby to put in these things."

"So soon?" muttered Joe in response.

Margaret didn't think the sentiment reflected the proper amount of enthusiasm.

"It's going to be OK, Joe. I'm a nurse after all, so I'll know what's going on. Oh!—another contraction!"

After timing it, she continued. "Wouldn't it be nice if the baby was born while Carol was there? I think she works today until three. But even if she isn't working, she told me she would come in."

Margaret chose the obstetrician and hospital on Carol's recommendation.

"I suppose her boyfriend will be coming to visit you too," Joe said glumly. "I'll have to think up some way to apologize to him."

"Carol already explained everything to him. I'm sure he understands. He really is a nice guy. I hope he and Carol decide to get married. It would be fun to do things together. I hope if they do get married, they don't wait too long to have children. It would be nice having kids near the same age."

Joe interrupted her abruptly by banging his fist on the table.

"You can't keep talking like this, Margaret! I already told you that I'm going to turn myself in to the police. I'm going to be in jail—don't you understand that?"

Tears brimmed in Margaret's eyes and she said, "I don't understand, Joe. Why do you have to turn yourself in? So what if someone from out of your past saw you. It could be nothing. Maybe it was somebody who just looked like him."

"You know that's not true, Margaret. People at work were questioned about me. Your parents got that phone call from someone wanting to know my address and phone number. I don't know if the police are involved or not, but Rod was the one asking questions at the hotel. If he wanted to talk to me, he could have earlier. He was trying to find out information about me."

Joe didn't want to see Margaret cry, so he stood up and held her in as close an embrace as the baby would allow. Terms of endearment did not come easily to Joe, but he searched for something to express his love.

"My darling Margaret, I'm sorry to sound this way, but I have to face the facts and so do you. Once I serve the time, I can get on with life, and if you wait for me we can pick up where we left off. But I can't be any good as a husband—or as a father—never knowing when I might get arrested. I'm tired, Margaret. I just can't run anymore."

Margaret struggled with her emotions as she replied, "Of course I'll wait for you. On our wedding day I promised to love you in the bad times as well as the good. But how soon are you going to talk to the police? Can you wait a few weeks?"

Before Joe had a chance to answer, Margaret stiffened and doubled over in pain.

"Another contraction. It's really strong. . . ."

Joe continued holding her while she counted time on her watch.

"It was a long one, too," Margaret said after it was over. "I think we better get to the hospital."

THIRTY-FIVE

MELISSA ANNE WAS JUST THREE WEEKS OLD, and despite her tiny size, she managed to draw the focus away from her parent's problems to her own presence. She was born with dark blue eyes, thick black hair, and strong lungs. Margaret enjoyed dressing her up in the frilly clothes her mother and sister brought, and putting matching bows in her hair.

Margaret's mother stayed for a few days to help out and enjoy her new role as Grandma, but was now back in Riverside. Although wanting to press Margaret and Joe regarding their future plans, Anne managed to keep the questions to herself for the time-being.

Margaret was concentrating on nursing and rocking Melissa and sending out birth announcements. Joe restlessly spent his days doing small projects around the house going for walks, or taking a turn at rocking Melissa.

For their one-year anniversary, Carol came over to watch Melissa so that Margaret and Joe could have dinner out. Margaret sighed as she looked at her reflection in the mirror. Only her largest dress fit her, and the belt made the bulge of her once-flat stomach more obvious.

"What do you think, Joe?" Margaret asked, turning so he could view the dress.

"It's fine," he said, barely glancing at her before focusing his attention once more on the television.

Disappointed with Joe's reaction, Margaret decided that a new dress was in order, one which would get the enthusiastic response she desired.

Joe's mood continued to be subdued throughout their evening meal. Margaret brought the want ads for Joe to look at, but he showed no interest. Then she talked about the plans her mom and sister were making for a baby shower, while Joe seemed absorbed with his food. Margaret attributed his distraction to being tired from "night duty" with Melissa.

After they returned home and Carol left, Margaret decided to broach Joe on the subject of his parents.

"Joe, don't you think your parents are hurt that you haven't called them yet? I'm sure that your aunt called your mom right away after we picked up my things. And I promised to let your mother know about the baby."

Joe looked uncomfortable. "I don't know if can face my father yet—or my mother. Or my brothers or sister for that matter. I don't know if they even want to hear from me after all this time."

"Your aunt seemed to think that they would be overjoyed to know where you were and to see you again."

"You don't know my father, Margaret."

"I got a good taste of him when I visited there—I know he's a hard man. But your mom is different. I'm sure she wants to see you. Do you want me to call?"

Joe slammed down a magazine in irritation that he had been holding, but then decided that Margaret was right.

"Go ahead and call. If anyone wants to talk to me, I'll get on the phone."

Margaret got out her phone directory and dialed the number.

"Hello, Isabela? Oh . . . Elena. Can you please get your mother? Hello Isabela, this is Margaret. Yes—he's here. He'll talk to you but he wanted me to call to make sure that you wanted to hear from him."

Margaret handed the phone to Joe.

"She really wants to talk to you."

Joe took the phone and nervously said, "Hello, mother?"

"José, of course I want to talk to you! How are you?"

"I'm fine, mom. The baby was born, and we have a little girl. Her name is Melissa Anne."

"A girl? How wonderful! I'm so happy! Can you come to visit or do you want us to come there?"

"Visit?" Joe asked weakly.

"How about tomorrow! It's Saturday."

"Um . . . I'll ask Margaret." Joe held his hand over the phone and said, "She wants to see us tomorrow!"

"Why don't we drive up there tomorrow, Joe. I feel up to it now."

"Mother? We'll come to visit tomorrow. We'll leave after breakfast. Can you tell me how—how father is?"

"He won't say it, but I know he's missed you terribly. He wants to see you, I know. I'm afraid he won't show what he feels, but he's been waiting to hear from you ever since I talked with Juanita. The others have been waiting anxiously, too. . . ."

The sunshine the next morning was in marked contrast to Joe's mood. Despite his mother's assurances, he dreaded the meeting with his family. The trip to Los Angeles was mostly in silence other than little noises made by Melissa.

When they pulled into the driveway, Joe wasn't out of the car before his mother came running out, with his sister and brothers trailing behind. His mother held him tight as tears ran down her face. Then she let go of him to embrace Margaret and to see Melissa. Elena, Manuel and Fransesco all gave him hugs in turn, and then Isabela introduced Margaret to her children.

Joe looked up to see his father watching from the doorway. When their eyes met, Ernst walked over to Joe and shook his hand.

"Why did you stay away so long?"

Joe decided not to take offense and said, "I thought I had to. But mother says that you wanted to see me again."

"It's been very hard on your mother not to hear from you for all these years."

As Isabela predicted, Ernst was cool, but Joe sensed that the anger he had felt so frequently from his father while growing up was absent from his voice and expression.

"Would you like to see Melissa?" Joe asked, leading his father over to Margaret.

Joe was surprised at the gentleness with which his father held his new granddaughter.

"Let's go inside," Joe's Mother said. "I've got some of José's favorite foods prepared, and we can visit while we eat. We've got a lot of catching up to do. . . ."

THIRTY-SIX

TWO DAYS LATER, JOE FELT HE COULD PUT IT OFF NO LONGER.

"I'm sorry, Margaret, but it's not going to get any easier if I put things off. You have enough money in the bank now to keep you at home for a few months, and you have your job to go back to when your maternity leave is up. I wish it was different. . . ."

Margaret would accompany Joe to the Los Angeles police station. They drove up to spend the night with Margaret's family. It was a somber hour as Joe explained to his in-laws that he was going to turn himself in to the police. Margaret's parents were disappointed to learn of Joe's decision, but understood Joe's motivation better than Margaret was able to. Neither Anne nor Tony spoke much, but rather listened as their daughter and son-in-law spoke their minds.

Anne watched Melissa while Joe and Margaret drove downtown together to the police headquarters. The building was a large steel and glass structure across from the city hall. They parked in the back, then walked hand-in-hand to the front entrance into a lobby area. They told the receptionist that they wanted to discuss some information regarding a crime with someone in charge. She pressed them for details, but Joe was resolute.

Joe and Margaret were directed to chairs in the lobby area, and waited impatiently for about fifteen minutes. Joe was just about ready to ask how much longer it would be, when a police officer came their direction. He appeared to be in his late forties and had a dour look on his face. They stood up to meet him, and introduced themselves to him.

"My name is Sergeant Harper and I understand that you have some information regarding a crime."

The sergeant minced no words, and made no pretense of friendliness.

"Yes, I do," Joe replied. "Is there someplace private we can talk?"

With a look of impatience, Sergeant Harper said, "Follow me to my office."

He turned and walked briskly to the elevator leaving Joe and Margaret to trail behind.

They went up two floors into a small office. Joe noticed that everything was in order as if clutter had been banned from the room. The sergeant sat down behind his desk and leaned forward expectantly.

Joe and Margaret sat down, and Joe began to speak.

"I want to talk to you because of a crime committed seven years ago near here. In an attempted robbery at a drugstore, a man was killed."

The sergeant just looked at Joe as if to assess him. Margaret nervously twisted her hands in her lap. Joe paused for a moment to focus his thoughts, then continued.

"My friend, Carl Milford, was arrested and convicted for the crime. I believe he's still in jail for it. But he didn't do it alone. I drove his van that night, and I took a gun from my father without his knowledge to use for the robbery. It was my idea—I dared him to do it. I've come here to turn myself in."

Sergeant Harper looked at Joe in disbelief. All he needed was another nut case interrupting his day.

"After seven years, you're confessing now?"

"You might not understand, but I just can't live with this hanging over me anymore," Joe responded.

Joe looked the sergeant in the eye with as much courage as he could muster. With resignation that he was going to miss his coffee break, the sergeant took out a notebook and pen from his desk drawer.

"Tell me the details of when and where this incident supposedly took place."

He jotted down the information, then told Joe and Margaret to wait in his office for a few minutes. Margaret reached over and took Joe's hand which was icy cold with anxiety.

"I love you," she whispered, as if fearful of being overheard.

Joe didn't respond with words, but gave her hand a squeeze.

After what seemed like an eternity, Sergeant Harper returned.

"I found record of the crime, and most of the details fit. However, Mr. Milford gave a written confession to the crime. He said that he was alone at the time and that he stole a gun to use for the robbery. He refused to say where he obtained the gun, and it was never found. He was identified in a police line-up by an employee of the store as being the person to commit the crime. The vehicle used in the robbery belonged to him and was identified by an eyewitness."

"But I was in the van!" Joe interjected. "I was driving that night because he was so high that I was sure we'd get into an accident if he drove."

"Mr. Bechmann, as far as the Los Angeles Police Department is concerned, this case is officially resolved. We have no reason to believe that a second person was involved in the crime. As far as I can tell, justice is being served with the guilty person imprisoned at a correctional facility."

Neither Joe nor Margaret knew what to say. They looked at each other, then looked at the sergeant.

"I can go, then?" Joe finally asked.

"There's no reason to stay," the sergeant responded dryly.

Joe rose and said, "Thank you for your time. I guess that's it then."

They went downstairs and walked to the car in disbelief.

"Does that mean you're free, Joe?"

"I don't know what to think," he responded. "I never thought this would happen. But I'm not in the clear yet. I have to talk to Carl. If he had evidence against me, he can have me brought to trial. There's got to be a reason that Rod was trying to track me down."

"Yes," said Margaret thoughtfully. "But there's also got to be a reason why he lied to cover for you in his confession. And after all you've been through to stay clear of the police, they don't care after all. There's got to be a reason for that, too. . . ."

THIRTY-SEVEN

JOE HAD TO SEND A LETTER TO CARL asking that his name be added to the visitors' roster. In the letter he simply stated that he wanted to talk, and would like to come on Carl's next scheduled visiting day.

Joe called the prison a couple of days later and found his name on the list. He kissed Margaret and Melissa goodbye, then made the three-hour trip to the state penitentiary.

"I'm here to visit an inmate, Carl Milford," Joe told the guard at the front gate.

After being searched and having to wait for a few minutes, he was escorted to the visitor's lounge. Carl was already there, standing near the entrance waiting for him.

"Hello José," he said warmly, extending his hand to shake. "I'm really glad to see you. I think we have some talking to do."

"I think so, too," Joe replied, not sure what to make of Carl's friendliness.

Carl escorted Joe to some chairs in the corner.

"Are you back in San Diego?" Carl asked.

"How did you know I left San Diego?"

Sensing Joe's suspicion, Carl said, "I better tell you first that I was trying to find you so that I could press criminal charges against you. Rod was helping me track you down."

"I thought that's what was going on when I saw Rod outside of work one day."

"You saw him?" Carl asked. "Is that why you left your job and your wife?"

"I knew something was going on when Margaret, my wife, got a phone call from someone asking questions about me. It must have been Rod. After I saw him following me I went to Mexico."

Carl was surprised. "But you're back in the U.S., and you're visiting me. Why?"

"I'm not sure I can explain it to you," Joe replied. "Margaret doesn't understand. She's glad I'm back, but she didn't want me to go to the police, and she didn't want me to come here. I went to the Los Angeles police to turn myself in, but you never mentioned me in your confession. . . ."

Carl looked uncomfortable. "I guess I just thought that's what a guy should do for a friend."

"But you're trying to bring charges against me now?"

"I was," Carl answered. "I thought you would turn yourself in when you heard about my arrest, and testify on my behalf. You were only seventeen, so you wouldn't get an adult sentence. I have to admit that I was very angry. When Rod told me that you left home, I decided to try to get even and—"

"I'm sorry about that," Joe interrupted. "I guess I wasn't thinking about you. I was scared and didn't want to face up to things."

"I can understand that now," Carl replied.

Joe continued, "It means a lot to me to think that you covered for me at your trial. I should have done what I could for you. But it's past now. Do what you have to do. I know I deserve it."

"I am going to do something, José, but it's not what you think. Do you remember the park by my parents' house?"

Joe nodded yes, puzzled by the change in conversation.

"In the northwest corner, there is a park bench with a tree and some bushes by it. Your dad's gun is buried in a plastic container between the tree and the hedge. Go dig it up."

"I don't understand," said Joe in puzzlement.

"That gun is the only evidence that you were involved with the robbery and murder charges. It is registered in your dad's name and your fingerprints are on it. I want you to take it because I'm not going to try taking legal action against you. I've forgiven you—and I hope you're willing to forgive me, too."

"Forgiven me?" Joe repeated in confusion.

"I want you to know that it got to the point where I hated you, and it was eating at me inside. All I thought about was somehow getting revenge. When Rod told me that you left San Diego, I really hit bottom. But then something happened—something really important. Even though I've gotten a lot of grief about it, I'm going to tell you something—God changed me."

"How?" asked Joe, incredulously.

"This guy, Robin, started visiting me through a prison program. He really challenged me to think about what I believed, and let me tell you that there's plenty of time to think in prison. Anyway, he told me that he was a Christian, and I gave him a hard time for a while. But when I saw that he was really serious about what he believed, I wanted in my life what he had in his. I prayed to ask God to forgive me for all the things I did that were wrong, and I know he did."

Carl ended with an emphasis that sounded as though he expected to be challenged. He had been under fire for his conversion. Leon Jackson, the guard, practically made it his mission in life to antagonize him. If it hadn't been for the chaplain and the prison fellowship group, Carl didn't think he could have handled things.

"How do you know He did?" Joe asked intently.

"The anger and hate is gone. So is the emptiness. I feel better than I ever thought possible."

"Did it happen all at once?"

Carl paused to think, then answered. "I know that God forgave me right away. But then I had to forgive other people, and that took a while. I still struggle with my temper, but when I ask God to help me, he does."

They sat in silence for a moment, then Joe said, "Thank you for what you're doing, Carl. Not just for my sake, but for Margaret's—and Melissa's. I've got a baby now, too. I'll come back again to visit. Would you like me to bring Margaret and Melissa to meet you?"

"I'd really like that, José. It does get kind of lonely here."

Joe shook Carl's hand.

"I'm glad for what's happened to you, Carl. And I'd like to renew our friendship. Maybe some day I can make up for things. . . ."

EPILOGUE

JOE HANDED THE MAN BEHIND THE COUNTER HIS DRIVER'S LICENSE and credit card. With leathery skin and a closely cropped white beard, the man looked the part of a fisherman.

"Here is the key and two life jackets. The boat is on the other side of the pier. Just look for the same number that's on your key ring."

Joe thanked the man, then took Margaret by the arm to walk to the boat he just rented.

"I'm glad he didn't say anything when we told him that we didn't want to rent the fishing rods," Margaret said.

"Don't worry about it," Joe responded with a smile. "I'm sure there are plenty of people who rent boats and don't go fishing."

As they climbed into the boat, Margaret asked rather doubtfully, "Are you sure you know how to run this boat?"

"We'll find out soon if I do or not," Joe cheerfully replied. "Of course, if the waves capsize us, I know how to swim."

"That does me a lot of good. I'll drown while you swim safely to shore."

Margaret enjoyed being at the beach, but had never ventured very far out into the ocean. She enjoyed the smell of the salt water and the sound of the surf while sunbathing and people-watching. The only boat she had ever been in before was a much larger one, on a cruise to Santa Catalina island.

The motor turned over and sputtered to life.

"Here we go!" Joe said over his shoulder to Margaret. "You better get your life jacket on."

"Believe me, it's on already!"

Suddenly Margaret wished that she had Melissa in her arms to help calm her nerves. She hoped that Melissa was being good for her mother. Margaret watched as the shoreline began to recede into the distance. Her hair began to blow in the breeze, so she tied it back with a hairband from her purse.

"Did I ever tell you why I learned how to swim?" asked Joe in a more serious tone of voice.

"No, you never did."

"Back when I was thirteen I almost drowned. I was on a summer youth camping trip. Carl and Rod were there, too. In the middle of the night we snuck out to go canoeing. We tipped the canoe over, and neither Rod or I could swim. We both panicked, and if it hadn't been for Carl . . ."

Margaret leaned forward and took his hand.

"He saved my life then, and I had the chance to help him out later on, but didn't. Now he's saving me a second time. I owe him a lot."

Margaret replied, "I think that what he needs from you is friendship right now. You can start repaying him in that way. When he gets out of jail he'll need a lot of help making adjustments. You can be there for him—maybe help him find a job or something."

Joe put the motor in idle.

"This looks like a good spot," he said. "I don't want to go out so far that we lose sight of shore."

"Do you really think this is the right thing to do?" Margaret asked.

"Enough people's lives have been harmed by it. I just want to be finished now," Joe replied.

Margaret handed him a plastic container. Joe opened it and took out his father's gun, which was wrapped in a cloth. He took the bullets out of the gun and threw them as far as he could. The engine noise and lap of the waves absorbed any sound they might have made. Joe picked up the gun, checking to make sure that the serial number was completely filed off. Then he threw the gun into the water as well. Sunlight glinted off it for a moment, then it hit the water with a small splash.

Joe pictured himself diving into the ocean with the gun in his hand, plunging down to the dark ocean depths, and burying it in the sandy bottom. He could almost feel the sensation of breaking through the surface of the water again, to the sunlight and air, free of his past.

"It's all behind me now," he said more to himself than to Margaret. "This time it really is a new beginning."

"I hope so," Margaret said in response. "I want to get on with life. I want you and me and Melissa to be happy together."

"You know what I still can't believe?" Joe asked. "Carl was happy. I don't think I've ever seen him that way before. He had a lot going for him. He was smart, had friends, and his parents gave him a lot. But I've never seen him so . . . at peace with himself—and he's in prison! He said that God changed him. I think I believe him. While I was in Ensenada, I met someone else who talked about God working in people's lives."

"God answered my prayers, Joe."

"How's that?"

"You're back home—where you belong."

Margaret squeezed his hand, then kissed it.

"Are you ever going to tell your father what you did with his gun?" Margaret asked.

"I'm not sure. I don't know if he cared more about what happened to the gun or what it was used for. I can't figure him out. He seems to be warming up to you and Melissa, but I don't know how he feels about me. He hasn't said much to me other than to say that it's about time I started being responsible. I don't know whether he means it as a compliment or an insult."

"Give him time, Joe. People change—you never know what the future will bring."

Joe moved to sit next to her. He gave her a lingering kiss, then pulled her against him, wrapping his arms around her in an embrace. Removing the hairband, he began to gently caress her hair.

"Whatever it brings, I know I can face it now. And I know it's going to be all right."